KISS ME IN
NEW YORK

KISS ME IN
NEW YORK

~ BY ~

CATHERINE RIDER

KCP
Loft

Kids Can Press gratefully acknowledges the financial support of the Government
of Ontario, through the Ontario Media Development Corporation.

Published in Canada and the U.S. by Kids Can Press Ltd.
25 Dockside Drive, Toronto, ON M5A 0B5

Kids Can Press is a Corus Entertainment Inc. company

www.kidscanpress.com
www.kcploft.com

The text is set in Minion Pro

Edited by Kate Egan
Designed by Emma Dolan

Printed and bound in Altona, Manitoba, Canada, in 6/2017 by Friesens Corp.

CM 17 0 9 8 7 6 5 4 3 2 1

Library and Archives Canada Cataloguing in Publication

Rider, Catherine (Novelist), author
Kiss me in New York / Catherine Rider.

ISBN 978-1-77138-848-1 (hardback)

I. Title.

PZ7.1.R53Kis 2017   j813'.6   C2016-906700-9

To Julia, for all the New York stories

~ CHAPTER ONE ~

CHARLOTTE

CHRISTMAS EVE 2:00 P.M.

A broken heart changes a lot of things. For example: I'm not *usually* the type of person who scowls when a smiling lady at JFK Airport wishes me "Happy holidays!" as she checks me in for my flight.

But right now, I can't help it. It's Christmas Eve, and I just want to get out of New York as fast as possible. I want to never look back. I want to forget I ever came here in the first place — forget that I ever thought I could find some kind of New Me in this city.

When I first got here, New York was all bright lights and excitement. But two weeks ago, that changed. I began seeing what Mr. and Mrs. Lawrence, my host family in Yonkers, always complained about whenever I brought up "the city" and how much I liked it. Like all the rude people — *so many* of them — and they always seem to be *in the way*. The rats. The fact that the entire city often smells like it's standing underneath a giant umbrella made of rancid pizza.

The lady's smile is morphing into a frown. I realize I must look totally weird standing here, scowling and staring into nothing. I try to

7

cover up by saying, "Oh, yes … you, too!" I tell her that I am catching the 6:45 p.m. flight to London Heathrow.

She looks at her computer, her brow creasing. "Wow, you're here with almost five hours to spare. You Brits like to be punctual, huh?"

What I would like to say, if it were socially acceptable and would not make me seem like a crazy person: "It's nothing to do with punctuality, Ronda." (That's the name on her badge.) "Up until two weeks ago, I was *so* not looking forward to going home. I was having the absolute best study abroad semester at Sacred Heart High, and I was starting to get ridiculously excited about coming back here for college in September. I'd been accepted — early admission — into Columbia's journalism program, and I was over the moon about that. Because I was going to be moving to a place where I could *live* stories. New York was going to give me so many things to write about. And I could become New Charlotte. Who's New Charlotte? Oh, New Charlotte is basically me — I mean, we look identical, because there's nothing I can do about that — but New Charlotte is impulsive and outgoing, where Old Charlotte was a bit more indoorsy. New Charlotte takes chances; Old Charlotte would never do that. And then, I actually came here and discovered, New Charlotte was bloody awesome! Lots of people liked her … especially this boy in my English class, Colin.

"But *then* Colin went and broke my heart. The minute that happened, I stopped being all impulsive and free, which gave me time to focus on the things that kind of suck about New York — like how your subway cars are about as comfortable to ride as shopping trolleys. And how you allow really, really dumb things to happen, like letting cars *turn into* crowds of crossing pedestrians! And how cold it gets here in December. Seriously, that's got to be some kind of human rights violation."

What I actually say: "I'm just eager to get home, I guess."

Which is no less true. Just a more direct way of saying what I *want* to say. Maybe that's why things didn't work with Colin. Maybe if I'd just come out with it, asked him if he was unhappy … If I'd been more direct, would we still be together?

Come on, Charlotte. Being more direct would not have made Colin any less of a bell-end.

I can't fault my own logic there, just like I have no response to my brain's cruel taunt — *This is what I get for trying to be impulsive.*

When my tote bag knocks over a Statue of Liberty model, which clips a toy taxi and sends it crashing down onto an Empire State Building statue below, I realize two things: one, my tote bag is as unnecessarily big as my mum has always said it is, and two, I must have checked in, checked my suitcase, walked away from the desk, through the airport and into a gift shop, without my brain recording the memories of doing any of these things.

But, yep, I have a full boarding pass tucked into my passport and am, for some reason, standing in a gift shop. What the hell am I doing here? I do *not* want reminders of my semester abroad — I want to leave everything behind. New York is welcome to everything it touched, everything it spoiled — everything it turned rotten.

I was not lying to Ronda. Right now, I just want to go home. Go home and settle back into being Old Me … No, not *old*. Original Me. The Real Me I apparently have no choice about being. Let's call her English Charlotte.

The sharp, hot prickles behind my eyes tell me it's time to get out of here — not even English Charlotte weeps in public — and so I weave my way through displays of soft statues and plastic skyscrapers, marching back out into the main airport building. I duck my head to avoid catching a glimpse of the giant posters of the New York City skyline — today, now that I'm in a bad (sad) mood, I don't see the bright lights of a city that never sleeps. I see tall, glass and steel monstrosities glaring at the sky as if challenging it to a fight.

Come on, New York — what did the sky ever do to you?

God, coming to the airport so early might have been a mistake — now I have four hours to sit around and mope. I stare at my mobile, checking Instagram every few minutes: first my timeline, then my comments and new follows, then my friends' activities to see who liked whose photos (refresh-refresh-refresh). My battery will be totally drained, and I won't even be able to spend the remaining time listening to music. But that might be a good thing — there's pretty much nothing left on my playlists except miserable songs.

I've actually started to really, really like The Smiths — and that's probably not a good thing in my state!

I need to be super attracted to the girl I'm with. I need to feel — I don't know, passion — I guess. And ... I just don't.

That's how he broke up with me.

I decide that distraction is what I need, so I march into the Hudson bookstore — no, no, book *shop* (no more American English for me!) — and come to a dead stop when I realize I'm not sure what I'm looking for. The bestseller chart is all chick lit, which I usually like — but, right now, all the hearts I'm seeing make me want to vomit. Then my eyes fall on a trio of trashy, pulpy, violent thrillers — now there's an idea. A book that's all plot, violence and *no feelings*. That seems like exactly what I need right now. I spend about five minutes making a choice, trying to predict how distracting each book will be, but it's hard to tell from the almost identical covers — silhouetted men posing mid-stride beneath one-word titles. I wonder, what is the difference between *Vengeance*, *Retaliation* and *Payback*, really?

Payback's tagline is, literally, "DONNY HAS IT COMING ..."

I don't know who Donny is or why he "HAS IT COMING," but I pick up the book and head to the counter, turning around and sidestepping a figure who's risking a dislocated shoulder to reach a hardback on a high shelf. One of the biggest bestsellers. I hear him grunt, then swear, as a different book falls from the shelf — I just about register that it's a small paperback before it bonks me on the head. I instinctively thrust out my arms, catching and cradling it.

"Oh, dude, I'm so sorry."

I look up into the deep brown eyes of a tall guy, who I guess is a couple of years older than me. His hair is long and shaggy and looks like it's been flattened by the beanie I can just tell he's been wearing for much of the day. I've been in New York long enough to recognize guys like him as Williamsburg Wankers — a nickname (okay, an insult) I coined myself and which the girls at Sacred Heart thought was just The Best and Most British translation of "hipster" they'd ever heard.

This guy might be a Williamsburg Wanker, but he's pulling off the scruffy and rough yet hygienic look quite well. Brooklyn hipsters don't have the same … *crusty* look that I see on hipsters back home. Even in my bad mood, I recognize hotness.

If I had a heart that hadn't just been used as a punching bag by another hipster with good cheekbones, it would probably be fluttering a little right now.

He's holding out his free hand. The other is holding whatever book he's here to buy and a bag from the same gift shop that I just left. "Want me to put that back for you?"

I look down at the two books I'm holding. The book I rescued from a painful death is covered with cartoon drawings of wineglasses, musical instruments, hearts with bandages over them — and, weirdly, a puppy. Swirling red letters scream at me:

Get Over Your Ex in Ten Easy Steps!

"Maybe try accepting that he's an asshole."

I look back up at Hipster Hottie, who's smirking as he glances from me to the self-help book. Then he points at *Payback*. "Though it looks like you're researching more violent ideas."

I nod. "I'll just daydream about paying him back."

"You should let me get that. After all, I almost gave you a concussion just now."

I hand him the book. "Thank you. You have earned yourself immunity from my Payback List."

Um, what's going on here? Am I flirting — with a stranger? This isn't exactly "like" me, but I guess since he's a cute guy I'm never going to run into again, there's no harm in flirting a little?

Even English Charlotte does that sometimes. And just because I've been reset to English Charlotte doesn't mean I can't add to and improve her. Hipster Hottie doesn't know that I was just totally dumped by my boyfriend for not being super attractive; doesn't know that I've been crying hourly for the past two weeks; doesn't know that my Autumn Mission to become a Daring Free Spirit resulted in that spirit getting arrested and thrown into an emotional dungeon.

The original New York mission is still active: for a few hours more, I *don't* have to be the shy, timid English girl.

I can be her when I get home.

"Hey," he says, tucking all the books under one arm, "can I get your opinion on something?"

He doesn't wait for me to answer. From the gift shop bag, he pulls out a pink teddy bear with a black T-shirt that has what looks like a child's drawing of the Manhattan skyline on it. In big, pink letters are the words "I HEART NEW YORK."

No heart symbol — the word "heart" is actually spelled out.

"I got this for my girl. She's coming home after a semester away in Cali … How cheesy do you think this is, scale of one to ten?"

"Seventeen."

He laughs. Too much. I wonder if his laugh would be quite this annoying if it didn't come right after his mention of the g-word put the brakes on my optimism.

Learn your lesson, English Charlotte, I tell myself as I numbly follow

Hipster Hottie to the counter. *Operation New Charlotte was a humiliating failure.*

He pays for my book, and I tune out whatever he's babbling about. I'm sure his "girl" is lovely and everything, but it's not like I want to hear all about how much she'll "dig" the irony of the cheesy T-shirt. Once he's paid, he hands me the bag with my book, and we walk out together, coming to a stop just outside the store. We've walked into a human blizzard, Christmas travelers hustling in every direction.

"Thanks for the book," I tell him, stuffing it into my tote bag.

He's about to respond, when we both start at the sound of a guy's voice — a high-pitched yelp that cuts right through the hubbub of airport noise.

"You want to break up? Are you serious?!"

Hipster Hottie turns around — I have to sidestep to see past him — and we both stare. A young couple stands face-to-face just outside Arrivals. The girl is a tanned blonde with annoyingly perfect curly hair, wearing a pretty fabulous white walker coat. She looks like she's not much older than me. The pale blue suitcase behind her tells me she's the one who has arrived. The guy is also around my age and wearing a light-brown field coat that's clashing horribly with the yellow-and-cream plaid shirt I can see underneath. Over one shoulder is a red backpack, but I don't see any airport tags. This isn't a young couple returning from somewhere; this is a young couple *reuniting* at the airport.

Well, they *were* a couple. And "reuniting" might be a stretch.

The girl has her hands clasped together, held tight to her chest. The universal gesture for *I'm so sorry.* The guy has let the hand holding a dozen red roses drop to his side as his eyes dart left and right, as though he's just been asked to figure out the square root of 23,213.

I think I wore the exact same look when Colin broke up with me.

I offer Hipster Hottie a grimace — the universal expression for

Awkward. But he's not looking at me — he's looking at the floor, shaking his head and saying, "She told him she'd see him after the holidays."

Bloody hell, *that's* the girl he's here to meet?

He looks at me, his expression similar to the one Mr. Lawrence got the day a plumber told him he would be calling "sometime between ten a.m. and four p.m." A look that says, *Can you believe this BS that I have to deal with?*

"She was going to take care of it then. But here he is, showing up to 'surprise' her and putting her in this awful situation. What a jerk, huh?"

He doesn't even say goodbye; he just walks over to the splitting couple, taking out the stupid stuffed bear and putting it on the girl's shoulder. She starts in surprise, turns around, gasps in delight. Then she grins and pulls him into a long, deep kiss, while poor Rose-Bearing Boy looks no closer to solving his maths problem.

I turn away from the bizarre scene and make my way toward Security, remembering something that Hipster Hottie said to me.

I have no problem accepting that *he's* an arsehole.

✳

2:55 P.M.

"Sir, I understand you're upset, but I am not responsible for the weather. If you want to take it up with someone, try God."

I've heard the lady at the gate say versions of this same line to four different passengers now, and I'm still hoping that my brain has just decided to mess with me by imagining a nightmare where reports of a possible blizzard have thrown JFK Airport into chaos.

When I get to the front of the line, I put my palm on the desk as if

I need it to prop me up, tell the lady my flight number and desperately hope my plane has special wheels with alien-tech tires that give it enough grip to charge down the runway no matter how deep the snow, taking me far, far away from here.

Taking me home.

Gate Lady looks at her computer. "Well, honey, the good news is that your plane is here at JFK. The bad news is it won't actually be leaving, due to …"

Then she launches into some sort of explanation, but I'm not listening because my head feels like it's been dunked under water, my ears full of this weird rushing noise that makes everything feel suddenly distant. The black peacoat I'm wearing, which Mrs. Lawrence bought me when the weather turned, feels like it's come to life and is strangling my whole body.

My flight home has been canceled.

I'm stuck here.

"What about the next flight out? Can't I be transferred? I mean, it's a red eye, right? It makes no difference to me if I land at eight in the morning, instead of six — I'm not going to sleep anyway. I never sleep on planes. I get too excited by traveling." I can sense that I'm rambling, and I know why I am — as long as I'm talking, I'm not crying.

I can't be stuck here. I just can't! I need to get home. My parents are waiting for me. In fact, my dad is probably checking the status of my flight right about now, and when he sees that it's delayed, he's going to freak out.

"Miss, I'm so sorry," says Gate Lady, making a face like it's breaking her heart to be the bearer of bad news to a stranger. I've seen her make the same face twice already. "But with the weather conditions, all our other flights to London have long waiting lists already … There's very little chance you'll get on a flight tonight. I'm so sorry."

She directs me to an enquiries desk, where another too-smiley lady stares at a computer screen for what I swear is five whole minutes, before telling me that the next flight she can get me on does not depart until 9:30 … a.m.

I will not be home with my family on Christmas morning. Instead, I will be here in New York — the city I love but just want to leave.

*

I have another one of those Lost Moments. It's who-knows-how-many minutes later, and I'm wandering back out into the main terminal. I've left my suitcase with the airline, and over my left shoulder I have my tote bag, which holds nothing except the thriller that Hipster Hottie bought for me, as well as a voucher given to me by the airline. It's for the Ramada Hotel, where I guess I'm going to hole up and spend Christmas Eve … *by myself.* I've never stayed in a hotel by myself before, and all of a sudden I feel very out of my depth. What if the hotel won't let me in without an adult? What if I end up *totally* stranded, caught between a hotel that won't take me in and an airport that won't let me leave?

This is the worst thing that has ever happened to me.

"You'll be fine, love. You always are."

I'm on my mobile, speaking to Mum. I want her to be totally freaking out, like I am, but Mum's always lovely and calm. She's actually known for it. Everyone calls her "Mellownie" — I've always thought that was the lamest play on Melanie there could possibly be, but now, at this moment, it feels like one of the funniest things I've ever heard in my life.

I plonk myself down on a bench, putting my face in my free hand. It doesn't do much to make me feel better, but the airport feels further away for a bit — less like it's closing in on me.

Mum starts to say something, but her voice is drowned out by Emma's, and I imagine my five-year-old sister fighting tooth and nail for the house phone. "Mummy, Mummy, I want to talk to Lot! Pleeeeease!"

When she was a baby, Emma could never get her mouth around "Charlotte," so "Lot" was what she settled on. Every other day of my life, I've found it annoying — but not today.

"Not right now, Em," Mum says. Then, to me: "Can't you go back to the Lawrences'?"

"No," I tell Mum. "They're spending Christmas with relatives in Vermont. They were driving there from the airport, after dropping me off."

"You'll be fine, love," she repeats. "You can go to your hotel and at least be warm and safe, right? What more can you ask for?"

I wipe my eyes and turn my mouth from the mobile so she can't hear me sniffle. There is a *lot* more that I could ask for than a warm hotel room — like, a flight out of this city of misery. *How about that for "more"?* God, why has my life decided to not just knock me down but also spit in my face and then run away laughing?

Mum tells me that we can all do Christmas on Boxing Day and that the whole family loves me and — for some reason — this chokes me up. We've never really been the most affectionate of families, and it's the fact that Mum feels the need to *say* something that underlines for me that, yep, this is a shitty situation I'm in today. I tell her I love her, too, painfully aware that my throat is strangling my vowels, and, before we click off, Mum tells me, "I want you to listen to me, okay, Char? You listening?"

"Yeah."

"I know this feels horrible, and I understand, but I don't want you wallowing or sitting around and getting upset. Yes, this is unfortunate, but it's not the worst day you could be having, all things considered. Right? There's always someone who's worse off than you are, love."

I tell her I understand — and I do, but I also know it will be a while before I can actually agree with her. We end the call, and I stuff my mobile in my tote bag. I know that most of the weight I can feel on my leg is from the thriller that Hipster Hottie bought for me, but the thing I feel most aware of is the voucher, for a hotel room I'm a little nervous about staying in alone. Mum was very mellow about that, too, insisting that if I can fly to America by myself, I can survive a night in a hotel room.

She's right — even English Charlotte should be able to get through that.

But I know that the room itself will be bland and basic — and probably beige. I'm getting depressed just thinking about it, and I know that the only thing I will do in that room is sit and think about Colin, the horrible thing he said to me and the look on his face when he said it — as if explaining why he was dumping me was a huge inconvenience to him or something. I'm going to think about how big an arsehole he is and feel like a total loser for wishing I *had* made him feel passion, or whatever it is that makes him super into the girl he's with. He's not worth the tears he has made me cry, and yet I'm starting to think that calling him and asking if we could have a time-out on this whole breakup, just for half a day, so I don't have to sit in a hotel room and think about him, actually seems like it *isn't* the craziest and most desperate thing I've ever considered doing.

And this is where I find myself on Christmas Eve, after my failed semester in New York — alone in an airport, with no way of getting home until tomorrow, the only thing to my name a pulpy thriller about some guy called Donny who, for reasons I'm caring less and less about, "HAS IT COMING." I reach into the bag for the hotel voucher, to double-check the address, and when I move it aside, I see not the cover for *Payback*, but instead …

Get Over Your Ex in Ten Easy Steps!

The bloody self-help book! Hipster Hottie must not have been paying attention at the counter. Seeing it right after I had the fleeting thought that I could call Colin to come to my aid makes my blood boil, and I reach in and grab the book, tossing it aside.

It's only as I toss it that I notice I'm not alone on the bench. There's someone strangely familiar sitting next to me. A boy, about my age, kind of tall, with close-cropped dark hair, wearing a brown field coat over a yellow-and-cream plaid shirt — not a fashion disaster, but they kind of don't go together. He's slumped, a dozen red roses in his lap, a red backpack between his feet, and so distracted that he doesn't notice my accidental Christmas present — paid for by the guy his girlfriend literally just ran away with — bounce off his scuffed hiker boots.

But I apologize anyway, as I lurch forward to pick it up. I should throw it in the nearest rubbish bin — but, for some reason, I hold it close to my chest.

His reaction is delayed, like my voice wasn't traveling at the speed of sound or something. He turns and looks at me with vacant eyes, and all of a sudden I get what Mum was talking about. Someone worse off is sitting right next to me. Okay, so he might be worse off *at the moment* only because his dumping happened almost literally just now, but still. I'd have felt a book hit my foot.

I think.

He turns away from me and stares into space again. I'm doing a brilliant job of helping the worse-off person, aren't I?

"I'm Charlotte," I tell him, picking up his hand and shaking it. "And *you've* had a lucky escape."

The poor sod just looks down at our hands, as if this is his first-ever handshake, then up at me, confused. *Good one, Charlotte* — while he was getting dumped earlier, he would hardly have noticed the nosy British girl nearby (who happened to be standing next to the guy who was about to make off — and out — with his ex, right in front of him).

I explain myself. "I, um, saw you before ... with your girlfriend."

He looks down at the roses. "Yeah ... Shoulda figured our little show would attract an audience."

He's talking, at least, and I almost laugh when I realize that I honestly have no idea what my plan is here — he's the worse-off person, but I'm hardly going to heal his heart today, am I? Plus, my own heart might not be gushing blood right now, but that's probably because it's got no blood left to bleed after what Colin did to me.

"What's your name?"

He talks to the roses. "Anthony."

"Hello, Anthony. Trust me — you had a lucky escape. She's ... bad news."

"You don't know her."

"I know enough to know that you don't want to waste your time on a girl who would actually dump you on Christmas Eve for the first handsome guy who came along."

Anthony half turns to face me, his wide eyes indicating his seriousness. "You don't understand what happened between us, okay? Maya's not some shallow bimbo who runs off with the first hot guy to come along and turn her head." He sounds convinced. But, from where I was standing, the second half of that sentence is dead wrong.

"She just ... she just ... probably hasn't been dealing all that well with the long-distance thing. She's been away for the whole semester, you know? She's only just started at college, it's all new to her — of *course* that's going to mess with her head."

He sounds convinced. But I spent time with the guy she made off with — he seemed like a real Williamsburg Wanker, which means he's from Williamsburg (or that general area), which means she was about as far away from him as she was from Anthony.

But I don't say anything. I don't have to, because Anthony puts his face in his hands and leans back in his chair. He clenches his fists and lets them fall into the unwanted roses.

"No, you're right," he says, finally. For a moment, I wonder if he's going to cry, but he takes a deep breath and shakes his head. "She did a shitty thing. And what's crazy is, if I hadn't shown up to surprise her, I wouldn't have known what was going on."

I feel an urge to reach across and squeeze his forearm. But I don't do that — I just tell him, "You should go home. Watch some dumb movies with your family, whatever's going to keep your mind off it. Whatever normal Christmas you were thinking of having tonight, have it."

"I can't go home," he tells the roses. "I told my family I was spending Christmas with Maya and her family — I thought, if I surprised her, she'd ..." He jumps from that thought to another. "If I go home now ..." He shakes his head. "Forget it. I just ... don't want to go home tonight." He notices me frowning at him. "What?"

I realize what my face must look like — the face of someone thinking, *Poor you*. "Nothing," I tell Anthony. "Just ... I know a little of how you feel. I had a breakup — about a fortnight ago. That means, two wee —"

"I know what a fortnight is," he tells me.

"Sorry. Anyway, whatever the problem is with your family, get over it. It's Christmas, and you get to be with them. It could be worse — you could be looking at Christmas Eve at the Ramada."

He makes a sympathetic face, then frowns down at my lap. For a second, I think he's leering at me, and I'm about to make a disgusted noise — getting dumped does not make that okay — when I realize that he's just looking at the book I'm still holding. "If I were you, I'd dump that in the trash on the way out of here."

"It was on the bestseller chart," I tell him. "It must be working for *some* people."

"'*Ten Easy Steps*'? If it was *one* step, I might trust it. Ten steps sounds like some kind of scam to me."

I look down at the book, turning it over in my hands. There's a small portrait of the author — Dr. Susannah Lynch — in the bottom-right corner. A middle-aged woman, with a style that's stranded between hippie and sensible/classy, and a pleasant, open face that seems to insist that she just wants to help every single person who buys this book.

"Yeah," I say, "I guess ten steps would take a while ..."

I look up from the book to Anthony. The two of us have been dumped. He doesn't want to go home, and I couldn't go home even if I wanted to. And I *really* don't want to go to the Ramada: that will only end in me curling up in a ball, crying, looking at my mobile every two minutes to check Colin's Instagram, because I somehow *need* to know what he's doing. What he's doing without me. His pretentious selfies in front of bus stops and subway stations — Colin's theme was his "journey" — used to make me cringe, but I'm suddenly much more interested in "where he's going."

I kind of hate that.

Before I can ask myself if it's a good idea, I'm asking Anthony how well he knows New York City.

He just looks back at me like I've asked him if he takes showers in cold custard. "I've lived here my whole life. What are you thinking?"

"I've got, like, seventeen hours until my flight. I refuse to spend all of them in a poky hotel room, staring at the walls. They're probably *beige*! I need to take my mind off my troubles — and going into the city on Christmas Eve will be great for that, don't you think? You don't know this, but I came here to live some stories, and I didn't really do that. But how many people get to write about being stranded three thousand miles from home on Christmas Eve?"

He's still looking at me, unblinking. "Probably none, because don't most of those people get mugged?"

"That's probably because they're by themselves." I don't know if this is English Charlotte or New Charlotte — but whoever it is, she has a plan.

Anthony's shaking his head. "No, no, no …"

"You *did* say you didn't want to go home," I point out. He starts to say something, then stops. He's got no answer.

Just a question. "You really think that wandering around New York is going to fix everything?"

Of course I don't, I want to say. I don't expect that wandering around Manhattan at night is going to fill in the cracks in my heart; it probably won't even paper over them. But I'm hurting, and I want it to stop. And I'm lonelier than I thought could be possible, and I don't want Anthony to go. I guess this is because he is the only person in New York City right now that I know (even if I only kind of, sort of know him). And if I at least come out of this trip with a Story, a unique experience — that I could have only in New York — then, maybe, just maybe, when I'm an old lady, I won't be kicking myself at how I wasted three months of my life on both a boy and a city that didn't love me back.

After all, old ladies probably get seriously injured kicking themselves. Arthritis and stuff.

"Come on," I say instead. "Come with me! It'll be fun. You look like you could use fun. I know *I* could."

But he's just shaking his head. "Kid, if you think getting over love is that simple, then …"

He trails off, shaking his head again. Smirking.

For some reason, this makes me want to hit him with his own unwanted roses. I think it's because he called me *kid*. "Then what?"

"Nothing."

"No, tell me — then what?"

He shrugs, shakes his head again. Picks up his roses and his backpack and stands up. "Then I guess you don't understand love."

He walks away, leaving me alone on the bench.

*

Ten minutes later, I'm standing at the back of a queue for taxis outside the airport. It's a *long* queue — the fallout from all the canceled flights. I am getting *snowed on*. I wonder if I'm some sort of idiot for ignoring the warm hotel room I've been given for free so that I can spend all night outdoors in winter.

But I'm determined that English Charlotte will go home with a great Story. A great memory.

My mobile, tucked away in my jeans pocket, buzzes against my leg. WhatsApp messages from friends back home, telling me they've heard I got stranded. The first two — from my best friends, Heather and Amelia, saying they're jealous I get to spend Christmas in New York — make me smile. But Jessica, the older of my two little sisters, has sent me a giant cryface emoji, which gives me legit sadface, and I stop checking the messages. I'll save them for later.

The sky is a gloomy gray, and snow is falling onto the stranded passengers in the long line. Shoving matches are happening up ahead, and a harassed-looking lady in a heavy coat starts patrolling the line, saying that they are going to get as many passengers into cabs as possible. She has a clipboard in one hand and is asking people their destinations, directing them to this cab or that cab. When it's my turn to answer, I realize I've not thought about where I'm actually *going*, but I'm remembering a neighborhood that the Lawrences took me to, where we had coffee so delicious I forgot that I missed good old English tea.

"Greenwich Village."

She looks at her clipboard, then points me to one of the cabs. She moves on to the next person in line, and I make my way. I open the cab's rear door, see who's sitting inside and groan.

"Oh, come *on*."

CHAPTER TWO

ANTHONY

3:40 P.M.

"You are such a douchebag."

"Oh, I'm a douchebag? Well, you're a passive-aggressive bitch."

The couple in the bench seat in front of us have been sniping at each other all the way from the airport to the Midtown Tunnel — but the words "douchebag" and "passive-aggressive bitch" seem to get them horny as hell. Now I have to listen to them try to choke each other with their tongues.

Me and Charlotte, the fuming Brit, share the rear seat, both of us staring at the roof. I wonder if her neck is hurting as much as mine is. We're sitting as far away from each other as possible, my unwanted roses between us. I don't know why I haven't thrown the damned things out the window already.

I'm not sorry for calling her out on her naïve attitude, but Charlotte was sweet enough to me in the airport that I *guess* I sort of feel bad for snapping and walking away from her like I did. I mean, that had nothing to do with her — it had everything to do with Maya.

Maya …

I must be a total idiot for not seeing it coming. Of course, couples can grow apart when one half is away at college on the other side of the country. But Maya didn't dump me for some Californian. She dumped me for what looked like a total DUMBO Douchebag — a guy also from Brooklyn, just a more *pretentious* Brooklyn. She was cheating on our long-distance relationship by having a long-distance *affair*.

She had to have known that guy before she left. And since she did know him, that means she's been cheating on me for a while. And if she's been cheating on me for a while, that means I *am* better off without her. I know that all of this is true …

So, why do I feel like I've swallowed a mouthful of broken glass?

The cab takes us into the city, and when we pass some dive hotel on Thirty-Ninth, the horny couple suddenly yells at the driver to stop. I guess they both must have roommates, or maybe they live with their parents. They give Charlotte and me apologetic looks, then throw a third of the fare at the cabbie, get out of the cab and wrap their arms around each other as they walk toward the hotel, giggling.

But one of them must say something wrong during the fifteen-feet walk from the curb to the hotel, because they start fighting again. I hear the word "ex-boyfriend" as the cab pulls away, and my chest clenches. That's what I am now.

Maya's ex.

The cab stays on Thirty-Ninth, heading west toward Hell's Kitchen, where I told the cabbie to take me. I wasn't planning on hitting Manhattan at all, but right before I got in the cab, I made the mistake of checking Snapchat and saw a post from Maya, at a coffee shop in Bushwick, announcing that she and this new guy, Ash, had "finally" agreed that they'd now be exclusive. From the angle of the video, and the way the frame wobbled continuously, I could tell it was shot on a selfie stick. *A goddamned selfie stick.*

For the briefest of seconds, I actually felt a little less shitty about getting dumped.

I decided that if Maya was hanging out in Brooklyn, I was going to take cover in another borough and hit up Ice Bar, on Fortieth Street in Manhattan. It's a total shithole, but my fake ID has never been questioned there — and Maya's not going to unexpectedly show up. She'd *never* set foot in Ice Bar. For one thing, its low lighting and drab color scheme make taking a decent selfie an impossible task.

Charlotte's going to the village — I guess she's hoping there's a Story there.

I'm rubbing the kink out of my sore neck. "That was kind of excruciating, huh?"

I don't know why I'm bothering to talk to her. The look she gives me suggests she doesn't really want me to.

"But I guess you Brits are so polite that, even if it got all Cinemax in here, you wouldn't say anything." I'm about to explain what Cinemax is, but she looks away from me. It's on me to keep the conversation going, I guess. "So ... how come the village?"

"Why do you care?"

"Well, I mean ..." What *do* I mean? Why did I ask that question? What does it matter to me where she goes? "I know you're supposed to be on a flight home right now. The village can't have been in your plans, and I know you're looking for a Story. What do you think you'll find there?"

"None of your business."

"Look, I'm sorry, all right?" Now she looks at me. "I was out of line, talking to you like that at the airport." I point to the damned roses, as if they're a replay of my humiliating breakup. "My head was kind of all over the place."

"Sounds like it still is."

"Maybe. I guess I'm bugging you a little because I'm worried. I don't like the idea of a young girl walking around the city alone at night."

She looks at me, her gaze softening, for a second. Then her eyes narrow and she turns away. "I can look after myself, thank you."

"I'm sure you can. Just … it's cold and dark. And if you're not from here, New York can be like … I don't know, some sort of monster. It might eat you alive, you know? Especially with that *Downton Abbey* accent you've got."

She makes an indignant noise, as though I've seriously insulted her. "I do *not* sound like —"

We both jump at the sound of a car horn blaring, because it comes from our cab, our driver. He mumbles a curse as he changes lanes, shaking his head at what I guess is the subpar driving of the cab just in front of us.

Before she can finish her protest, I raise my hands in apology. "I just meant, for anybody, it's not the smartest idea to be wandering around the city at night, waiting for something to happen. Because most likely, whatever happens is going to be something bad. Trust me, I have cops in my family. At least think about what you want to do — that way, you know, you … stay out of trouble."

Charlotte sighs and reflexively tucks a lock of her wavy dark hair behind her ears. The rhythmic, slowly sweeping glow of the street-lights we pass illuminates her face — I can tell her pale complexion is a year-round look, not just a winter one. She takes out the self-help book. She turns it over in her hands.

"Yeah," she says. "You're probably right. I admit, I haven't thought too much about *what* I was going to do. I just wanted to keep my mind off …" She doesn't finish, and I guess she's trying not to think about the guy who dumped her. "I've just never been away from home at Christmas before, and if I'm going to be spending it alone, half the world away from my family, I may as well make a Story out of it."

She keeps saying that. I'm starting to wonder if she actually means it, or if she's just trying to convince herself.

I point to the book. "What's Step One?" She squints at me, like, *What does that have to do with anything?* I explain: "There are ten steps in that thing, right? So, I'm guessing, there are instructions, suggestions: they might *give* you something to help get you started. Maybe …"

Charlotte opens the book and turns to the first chapter. She lifts the book really close to her face, because it's dark inside the cab, which is starting to finally pick up some pace. She reads aloud: "'Do something you stopped doing because your ex didn't like it.'" She flips through that section, skimming whatever else it says, then closes the book and shakes her head. "I was only with him for a term — a semester. I might need time to think on that one …"

I can feel the smile on my face as I think to myself that, maybe, I can help her with that. Because I don't need long to remember that there was something *I* stopped doing because Maya insisted that it was nonnegotiable.

I don't give myself any time to question whether this is a good idea or a bad one. "You hungry?"

I. DO SOMETHING YOU STOPPED DOING
BECAUSE YOUR EX DIDN'T LIKE IT.

We all "tweak" or "modify" our personalities a little when starting a new relationship. That's just natural. But before you know it, you've totally and utterly given up on a hobby or stopped eating a favorite food. While you're loved up, you can make your peace with this because you're doing it for your partner, to make them happy.

But now, that partner is an ex …

✳

4:05 P.M.

I redirect the cab to Bleecker, and we get out at John's — which, I tell Charlotte, serves the best pizza in Manhattan. I start to walk toward the entrance — then realize there's a question I should have asked before I told the cabbie to stop here.

"You like pizza, right?"

She nods, makes a face, like, *Are you serious right now? Of course I like pizza. Who doesn't like pizza?*

We take a step toward John's, and then *she* stops. "Your roses."

I turn and see the cab's taillights disappearing down Bleecker. I shrug. "Maybe his next fare will be a guy in need of an emergency Christmas gift."

Ten minutes later, we're two bites into our shared pizza, and I'm regretting playing it safe and ordering a medium.

"This isn't bad," she says, between chews, unaware of the stringy strand of mozzarella hanging from her bottom lip. I gesture to her chin, and she wipes her mouth with a napkin, muttering thanks and grinning.

I don't think Maya would have found that funny. Thinking about it, she'd have gotten mad — and probably found a way to blame me. But then, she'd never eat pizza, so this scenario would never happen — so I should *not* be thinking about it.

Charlotte takes another bite, this time much more carefully. She looks at the wood-paneled walls, where hundreds, maybe thousands, of New Yorkers have scratched graffiti over graffiti. Names, shout-outs to certain neighborhoods. One diner even left a phone number.

"I wonder," she says, in between chews, "who was the first customer to think, 'You know what I'm going to do? I'm going to etch something on the wall.' And what did they write?"

I shake my head, still reviewing the graffiti. More names, letters dug deep into the wood like open scars, are around one of the framed photos hanging on the panel: a black-and-white shot of a young couple, walking hand in hand down some street downtown. Just above it, some asshole had scratched the word *LOVE*.

I look away, back to Charlotte. "No way to know now, I guess. People have probably been scratching at the walls here since FDR was president. Maybe before."

"I guess that's one thing that never changes."

"What is?"

She raises a finger at me, signaling that I should sit tight and wait for her answer, because she's literally bitten off more of her slice than she can chew. After about ten seconds, she's still nowhere near finishing, and she rolls her eyes and shakes her head. I get the feeling that she'd smile if she were capable of doing so with a mouthful of pizza.

"What never changes," she says at last, "is people reaching out to other people." She gestures at the wall. "I mean, the thing that all of this ... graffiti ... has in common is that each one was made by someone who wanted someone else to listen to them. Doesn't matter if it's someone in particular" — she reaches up high and taps a fingernail against one of the etchings, the name *Robyn* carved deep into the panel, then her hand falls to just above the table, to a random phone number — "or potentially the whole neighborhood. Everyone who wrote something on this wall probably just wanted *someone* to listen to them."

I decide not to reply to that, because I can think of only one thing to ask: Is that how she feels? The guy who dumped her, broke her heart — was that his problem, that he didn't listen? Didn't *hear* her?

Charlotte puts down the remains of her slice, wipes her hands on a napkin. "So, your girlfriend made you give up pizza? That's rough."

"Not just pizza," I tell her, picking up my second slice and kind of hoping she doesn't want more than two. *Total* fail ordering a medium. "Meat, dairy and eggs."

"Are you serious?"

"She's vegan. Well, she has been since she went to college. Insisted that I support her."

"What a load of bollocks." I have no idea what "bollocks" means, but it makes me laugh and wince at the same time. British curses are so freaking cute, the way they sound PG and R-rated all at once. "How was she going to police that, if she was all the way in California?" She picks up another slice, takes a big bite.

"When we'd be on the phone, she'd say she could hear the meat in my voice."

Aaaand now we have a choking situation. But just as I'm making to stand up and ask if anyone in John's knows the Heimlich, Charlotte waves a hand at me to sit down.

"I'm fine," she says, wiping tears of laughter from her eyes. "I'm fine. Just ..."

"What a load of bollocks?" I venture. She's laughing again, and I hold up my hands in apology for putting her at risk a second time. Then I think, *Wait.* "Did I say California?"

She pauses, mid-chew, face frozen. Her voice is muffled by a mouthful of pizza. "You must have done. Either that, or I made a lucky guess."

I nod, finish my second slice and decide that now's the time she starts writing this Story of hers. Either that, or I just really, really want to change the subject. "Come on, then, English. You must have thought of a Step One by now."

She ponders this, shrugs. "The only thing I can think of is biking. Back home, I'd ride my bike everywhere, but when I got here, I was a little uncertain. You know, what with you lot driving on the wrong side of the road and everything. And I've never been that coordinated anyway, so I was nervous at first. But I was going to at least give it a try, because I loved it — and I hate the subway — but Colin was like, 'Hell, no, it's too dangerous. New York drivers don't give a …'" She grimaces and shakes her head. "Never mind. Yeah, cycling would be the thing. If I take up my spot at Columbia, I'd like to be comfortable riding around Manhattan."

There are three slices of pizza still on the plate between us, but, suddenly, I'm not all that hungry anymore. I reach under the table for my backpack, heavy from the spare clothes I brought with me, because I was expecting to spend the holidays with my girlfriend and her family.

"Come with me."

✻

4:35 P.M.

I'm leading Charlotte down Bleecker, which is more deserted than I've ever seen it. The bare tree branches are dusted white with snow, which is falling heavier now, so the storefront awnings shield nobody. All the un-dumped people are heading back to girlfriends, boyfriends, wives, husbands, I guess. Taking partners home to meet the parents, seeking approval, making things official. That's what I was supposed to be going through tonight. I was supposed to be among the people *not* on Bleecker right now. I should probably get out of the cold, go home and hang out with my family, but I just can't face them, because I know that my dad will go out of his way to hold up this incident as proof of the thing that he's always saying to me.

You just ain't got Luke's street smarts, Anthony.

He never says this to belittle me or anything — my dad has just always thought of me as a little too imaginative — too soft — for the big, bad world. But the worst thing? Tonight, he would be right. I *have* to be a moron not to have seen that Maya was bad news. So, no, I'm not going home just yet, and if this Stranded Brit wants to run around trying to write herself a great Story to help her get through a breakup, I have no problem with that.

Maybe it'll help me get through mine.

"Where are we going?" Charlotte asks.

"You'll see."

I stop at Bleecker and Mercer, pointing to the Citi Bike station, which is full, twenty or so blue bikes. Christmas Eve.

"Are you winding me up?" Charlotte raises her eyebrows at me. I notice that she actually *has* eyebrows — Maya's were so thin they sometimes looked like a trick of the light.

"Why not? It was something you stopped doing, right?"

"Munching on a meat feast and risking death on a Boris Bike are not the same thing."

"Who's Boris?"

"Doesn't matter. The point is" — she pivots to gesture to the traffic, which is kind of stop-start right now, bumper to bumper — "it looks a bit dangerous."

"So, we'll wheel them up to the bike path by the Hudson. The only traffic you have to worry about will be other bike riders. Come on, what do you say?"

She looks from me to the row of bikes, then down at the sidewalk. She's frowning, so I hit her with the thing we — kind of, sort of — have in common.

"You want to kill time, right?"

She nods. No frown — she's thinking about it.

I cock a thumb in the direction of the bikes.

"So, come on, then … Let's ride this out."

She rolls her eyes, groans, leans her head back — but she's grinning, snowflakes nestling in her cheek dimples.

"That was so bad," she says with a laugh. "But all right, why not?"

I rent the bikes, and we walk them along the cobblestoned streets to the West Side Highway, which we could *not* do on a normal day, because we'd be a hazard to pedestrians. But on Christmas Eve, it feels like we have the downtown area mostly to ourselves. At the bike path, I stop, get on, look to Charlotte.

"You ready?"

She hooks her tote bag over one of the handlebars, then swings her leg over the saddle. She looks a little … not nervous but uncertain. I can tell it's been a while.

"I suppose so," she says. "But you'd better take the lead, at least at first."

And so I set off, guiding her along the path. Every six or seven pedals, I can't help looking over my shoulder, to check that she's still with me, that she hasn't wiped out.

"Getting the hang of it?" I call, after we've ridden about six blocks.

"Yeah!" she calls back. "It's just like riding a bike."

I slow to let her draw level. "We're tied at one for lame jokes."

She winks at me. "Where are we heading?"

"I dunno," I admit. "I was just riding. Wasn't thinking too much about where."

"Didn't you say earlier that wandering around aimlessly was a way to get in trouble?"

"Yeah, for you," I tell her, "because you don't know the city. But me, I can wander just fine —"

"On your left!"

The voice is almost simultaneous with the bike that appears from nowhere, flying past Charlotte — on her left. It startles her, and she swerves right, wrestling for control, but I can tell that she's going to topple over. I reach for her with my left hand, taking a handful of her sleeve to help her stand while our bikes collapse beneath us.

It all happens in probably less than two seconds, and I'm now very aware of how tight I'm holding her, how close we're standing, how heavily we're both breathing. She's looking up at me, her face frozen, startled, and the fact that I have no idea what to say makes this whole thing even more awkward than it probably should be, so I take a big step back from her …

… and trip on my fallen bike, landing right on my ass. I curse, then I laugh. What the hell just *happened*?

Charlotte's laughing, too, and reaching down to help me up. "What was that you were saying?"

"Okay, never mind." I stand up, shake off. Stare down the path, but the speed demon that caused this mess is long gone. "The city's dangerous for everyone. Hope that didn't scare you off."

She shakes her head. "Definitely not. I'm just getting the hang of it. But maybe we should actually decide where we're going?"

I look down at Charlotte's tote bag, beneath the fallen Citi Bike. "What's Step Two?"

Charlotte follows my gaze, then shakes her head. "You don't have to —"

"Come on. You want to kill time, I want to … All right, not kill time, but I've got no place to be. Why not?"

She looks at me for a long moment, and even though her face seems to say, *You're a bit weird*, I feel like she understands. She's been dumped, too. She gets it.

She crouches and digs the bag free. Takes out the book, finds the right page. Smiles, screws her eyes shut and gives me a look, like, *You're not going to like this.*

"Macy's is on …?"

"Thirty-Fourth Street," I answer.

Charlotte stuffs the book back into the bag, then picks up her bike. "Well, that's where we're headed."

"Why?"

She rehooks the bag and swings her leg over the saddle. "Make-overs, of course. Race you there!"

And now she's pedaling away, and I'm watching her go, snowflakes dancing around her. A stranded British girl, riding a bike to Macy's on Christmas Eve, for a makeover a book is telling her is a good idea if she wants to get over her ex. Could this night get any more random?

But I'm leaning down to pick up my bike.

For some reason, I'm kind of curious to find out.

1. DO SOMETHING YOU STOPPED DOING BECAUSE YOUR EX DIDN'T LIKE IT.

CHAPTER THREE

CHARLOTTE

2. *EXPLORE ALTERNATIVE YOUS ...*

Having modified or tweaked your personality to meet the demands of a relationship over months or even years, it is very easy to lose sight of who you were before it began. But rather than just go back to Who You Were, what about exploring different options for Who You Are Now?

5:05 P.M.

I know it's embarrassingly touristy of me, but I can't help it — the windows at Macy's, with their intricate Charlie Brown display, are so magical, I actually gasp.

"It's not as good as last year's," Anthony mumbles.

"Come on." I point to the window that we're passing. Charlie is complaining that Snoopy's Christmas decorations are "too commercial." It's totally bonkers and totally Christmassy! "You're not impressed by this?"

"Last year's was better."

I wonder if he means when he was with Maya. Were they together this time last year? Anthony has been wearing this face — tight-lipped, narrow-eyed, like he's trying to will away a mild headache — since we docked our Citi Bikes at Broadway and Thirty-Second Street, and it's only now I realize that maybe his ex has been on his mind.

It's another moment where a distraction is needed, so I tug his coat sleeve and point out: "*They* seem to be loving it, though."

"They" are the two boys and one girl — siblings, which I can tell from their near-identical puffer jackets and beanie hats — pressing their mittened hands right up against the glass, their breath fogging it up as they gawp at the display. One of the boys, no older than six, turns around and looks up at the thirty-something couple standing, shivering, just behind them. "Mommy?" he asks. "Is Macy's where Santa gets the toys that he gives to the kids around the world?"

The mum gives the dad a bit of a panicked look as she stutters. "Um, yeah … I guess so, sweetie."

The boy frowns, looking suspicious, and the mum grimaces a little, seemingly wondering if this is the day the magic will die.

But her son just shrugs and turns back to gawping at the display. "He should hurry and pick up all this stuff, then. It's gonna be Christmas soon, you know!"

I look to Anthony, expecting to see him melting as much as I am — but when he sees me smiling at him, Anthony seems to realize that *he's* smiling and looks away from me.

No, no, no, I think. *No clinging to your misery. You're tagging along because you want to get over it. So, get over it!*

I gently nudge his shoulder with mine, urging him toward the revolving door, and he moves along. But outside the Thirty-Fourth Street entrance, he comes to a stop, looking unsure about whether he wants to go in. That's when I notice the ocean of people inside, making the airport crowds from earlier look calm and civilized.

Anthony tugs at my sleeve, guiding me toward the revolving doors. "Come on, let's get this over with."

About seventeen seconds later, I'm rethinking my approach to Step Two, because as soon as we go through the revolving doors, the chaos of Christmas Eve in Macy's hits me like a slap in the face. Children are running and screaming, but so are parents, chasing and screaming after *them*. The sight actually brings me to a standstill — for about two seconds, because more shoppers are streaming into the store, and one of them knocks into me. I lurch forward, and it's only Anthony's quick thinking, as he yanks back on my arm, that saves me from becoming part of a three-way tug-of-war over a fancy perfume gift set!

As the "tuggers" — three thirty-something guys dressed identically (brown sweaters, glasses, corduroy trousers) — argue over who saw the gift set first, I wonder if the makeover is really worth all this hassle and stress.

The gift set hits the ground with a clatter and a smash, and the Brown Sweater Trio leaps back, away from the mess. Given the over-powering citrusy scent that seems to replace the oxygen on the ground floor, I think their girlfriends, fiancées or wives have had a lucky break.

Now Anthony's pulling me toward an elevator bank, guiding me inside. He pushes the button for the eighth floor. "Why are we going to the eighth?"

"Because," he says, as the elevator gets moving, "Santaland should be closing up about now, so the eighth floor is most likely dead. We can take a breather, and then slowly descend into the madness."

At the eighth floor, the elevator pings, the doors slide open and I see that Anthony was right. It's pretty dead up here. There are a few older people looking at houseware stuff, some women shrugging themselves out of perfectly fine winter coats to try on new ones — but other than that, it's quiet.

In the center of the floor is Santa Claus. All right, not the real one — obviously — just a guy in a suit lugging a snow-dappled sleigh as Santaland shuts down for the day and for the year. His face is so stony I'm actually surprised that the ground floor isn't overrun with bewildered little kids asking if they'll be getting presents at all, because Santa seems so *angry* this year.

As Anthony and I share an amused look, a mobile rings, and Santa almost jumps out of his suit, patting himself down and muttering, "Where is it, damn it?"

One of the elves steps forward, reaching into a satchel slung over his shoulder. He takes out a roll of faux parchment and then a mobile phone, which he holds out. Santa pulls down his white beard — revealing a clean-shaven face — and glares at the elf.

"You stole my phone?"

The elf looks a little flustered. "You asked me to hold it for you, remember?"

"Oh yeah, like I'd ever do that."

"You did, George — you have no pockets in your suit, and you didn't want to miss the call if it was" — he gives the phone a little shake — "you-know-who ... calling."

Santa lets his beard snap back into place, taking the phone and staring at the screen. He gasps and looks up at his little helper. "It's really him," he croaks. Then he taps the screen to answer the call, turning away. "Giovanni? Oh, Gee-Gee, I'm so glad you got my messages ..."

He disappears into the Au Bon Pain restaurant, and I actually think, *Ugh, even* Santa's *love life is in better shape than mine.* Then I grin, wondering what Mrs. Claus would make of him having a Gee-Gee on the side.

I shake my head and tell myself to get back to business. But I've been to Macy's just twice, and one of those trips lasted only about eight minutes, because when we got up to the Mezzanine, Mrs. Lawrence saw her old high school boyfriend lurking among the handbags and she got us out of there. Thirty years later, and she was convinced he wasn't over her. Apparently, he'd friend-requested her from a second Facebook profile using his mother's maiden name. Creepy.

That's one good thing about me going half the world away — I won't have to worry about bumping into Colin in John Lewis. Ever.

It's only now that I realize Anthony is talking and has actually moved to stand by a color-coded map of Macy's. I walk over, apologizing. He taps the map, then points out a pair of escalators that he says will take us down to the seventh floor. It's only as we get on the escalators that I notice they're made of *wood* and make a weird clickety-clackety noise that has me worried they might collapse. But I do like how Manhattan seems content to just let ghosts of its past barge in on the present, like a stubborn older relative making sure the rest of the family doesn't forget them. It reminds me of home, because London's like that, as well. Maybe that's why I fit in so well here.

Not that that matters anymore, but it's a nice feeling to have on my last day.

Once we're on the seventh floor, I look around to see if any sales clerks are free, but the seventh floor is *much* busier than the eighth. Like, *The Walking Dead* is real-life-from-tomorrow busy!

"The sales clerks all look slammed," I tell Anthony.

He nods. "Guess we're on our own."

We walk to the nearest display table, which has a pyramid of folded black jeans. I'm about to pick up a pair when I see the price tag. $165? I maybe should have read more about Step Two — I didn't anticipate it being this expensive.

"Don't worry about it." I look at Anthony. A smile is straining to break free of the rest of his face. He'd probably be handsome if he

42

smiled more — it's only because he hasn't smiled much that I don't know for sure.

"It's a hundred and sixty-five dollars! For *jeans!*"

"Don't worry about it," he says again.

I reach into my bag and take out *Ten Easy Steps* ... flick through it.

"What are you doing?" he asks.

I stop on Step Two. "Looking for where it says, 'Shoplifting's totally fine and acceptable.' Nope, don't see *that* in the book!"

He's smiling now, and I was right — he looks better when he's relaxed. "I didn't mean that. I have a Macy's credit card — so, whatever we buy, we can wear today, and I'll return it after Christmas. Free makeover."

Buying clothes to wear for only one day — a few hours — isn't like me, but I can't pretend that getting to wear something expensive without paying for it isn't exciting. I'm about to nod, say all right, when I cringe at another thought. "This place *must* have, like, the strictest return policy. And it's cold and snowy out — no way we'll be able to keep these in returnable condition."

He rolls his eyes at me. "Stop being so British. New Yorkers don't always follow the rules. You're gonna need to learn that if you want to be one of us." He's walking past me, back to the escalator. "Now, I'm going down to the fifth floor to pick something out. Meet you there in ten?"

But something else in the book catches my eye, and I turn and walk to him, pulling him away from the escalator. "Nope, *I'm* going down to fifth."

"Why?"

"Because" — I show him Step Two, pointing to the text in question — "'letting a friend pick your outfit is a healthy exercise in seeing how people truly see you.' Besides, if I have to choose my own stuff, I could be here until Easter. It'll be much quicker if you just pick something out for me."

He steps toward me, and, for just a moment, I think he's going to take my hands in his and pull me away from the escalator. "Oh no, that's a horrible idea," he says. "Look at me — I don't have a clue about fashion."

I try to keep my eyes off the yellow-and-cream plaid shirt that really doesn't belong beneath the brown field coat, try not to show that I kind of agree with him. "It'll be easy," I say. "Just pick out something that you think you'd like to see me in."

Oh, that came out wrong. *Am I blushing? I feel like I might be blushing.* I quickly turn and start heading down the escalator, calling back that I'll be doing the same for him.

Yeah, I'm definitely blushing.

✱

5:25 P.M.

I'm feeling pretty confident in my outfit selection by the time I see Anthony coming down the escalator to the fifth floor. He doesn't look anywhere near as confident as I feel. He's holding a bundle of clothes tight to his chest like it's a newborn he's afraid of dropping.

"You ready to do this?"

"You sound like we're making a drug deal," I joke.

A smile breaks through his face, and his eyes light up. He fakes looking for cops. "I got your stuff here, girl, but you better get to steppin' before the pigs spot you."

I look at the floor so he doesn't see the silly grin on my face. Then we exchange the outfits in the least stealthy way possible, and we both laugh. I wish I was better at improv because, if I was, I could keep this little role-play going.

But I'm *not* good at improv. I only ever got B-minuses in Drama.

Signs direct us to changing rooms on opposite sides of the floor. "Meet you back here?"

He nods. "Sure."

We give each other a last look, as if we're about to jump off a cliff or something. Looking at each other just makes this awkward, so I turn and head for the women's changing rooms before I can think too long about how we are doing something totally ridiculous.

It's only after I'm in the booth and have laid out Anthony's selections that I actually see what he's picked out for me. Skinny, slightly distressed black jeans; a black T-shirt with a skull on it; an indigo scarf; a black leather jacket.

Who's he trying to turn me into, Jessica Jones?

But at least he seems to be thinking about what I'll be comfortable in, rather than what will look "hot," which was basically how Colin judged everything I wore. But then, I'm Anthony's one-day-only friend, and there's not going to be a time where we're seen together. No point where I'll be part of whatever front he wants to present.

My makeover is about *me*, not about Anthony *and* me.

It feels good.

Two minutes later, I've changed into the jeans and the T-shirt, and I look at myself in the mirror. The jeans are snug and in need of breaking in, but I have to admit, they look good. The skull on the black tee looks like it's in an intense staring match with its reflection, and with my dark hair I'm surprised I'm somehow managing to stop short of Goth. I complete the outfit by slipping on the scarf and then the jacket, expecting to see a ridiculous Bizarro Charlotte looking back at me from the mirror.

But I don't think that. I look ... all right, I think. Kind of quietly tough. Not "tough" as in "a girl who gets into fights" or anything — more the kind of girl who doesn't *have* to get into fights, because people know she doesn't tolerate nonsense.

I like her. I'm wondering what it was about me that made Anthony choose this outfit, and for some reason I think of the *Ten Easy Steps* book. As if it might have an answer. There's something niggling at me, something that caught my eye when I was in the taxi, flicking through the book for the first time … I take it out of my bag, flip to the contents page, my eye immediately drawn to Step Nine …

9. SEE YOURSELF HOW SOMEONE ELSE SEES YOU.

Mirrors often lie — and the mirrors in our minds are the emotional equivalent of fun-house mirrors, made out of a magical glass that we can alter, whenever we want to get down on ourselves. It is in the eyes of others that we see the parts of ourselves that we sometimes willfully ignore …

I don't know if this counts as crossing Step Nine off, but let's see how it goes — if I can get comfortable in this gear, then maybe Anthony's onto something!

I stuff my old clothes into my tote bag, step out of the booth and meet him in the middle of the floor. He's wearing the ensemble I selected: a pair of classy plaid trousers and a navy blue jum— *sweater*. He looks self-conscious; his shoulders are what my friend Amelia calls "slunched" — slumped and hunched at the same time. He has his red backpack in one hand, dangling loosely by his legs.

"You look nice," I tell him. I mean it. He does — apart from the slunching.

"This doesn't look very *me*."

I roll my eyes. "You do realize what 'makeover' means, right? It means, you try something different."

"You sure I don't look like a complete dork?" he asks, lifting a hand to rub the back of his head. I know this is a nervous tic of his, as I've seen him do it a couple of times already, and am surprised I've picked up on it. It usually takes me years to spot friends' "things."

"Oh, stop it," I tell him, giving him a playful slap on the arm and turning him around so that we're both standing in front of the full mirror propped up against a pillar. I stand beside him as we check out our reflections. "You look good."

And so do I. I notice that our selections for each other are very different. I came out rough and tough; he came out classy.

We're making eye contact in the mirror, looking at each other, but at the same time *not*. It's somehow more intense than actual, for-real eye contact — like the mirror is a third person in the conversation, cradling our gazes in its hands, threatening to drop them at any moment.

"You've just got to wear it like it *is* you," I tell him, putting one hand on his shoulder to de-slunch them, the other at the small of his back. "Confidence sells any look on anyone."

My fingertips brush the waistband of his trousers, and I freeze, thankful that I'm not looking at him looking at me in the mirror and that my hair is hanging over my face, because I'm *sure* that I've started to blush again. What's that about?

It's only weird if you make it weird, I tell myself. *It's a makeover — touching clothes is an occupational hazard.*

I realize that while I've been having my little freak-out about whether or not it's okay for me to be touching him, I've not actually stopped touching him. So I bring both hands together and smooth out nonexistent creases from the back of the sweater.

No big deal. Totally not weird.

I dare to look in the mirror. He's not looking at me — he's looking at the New-ish Him, his face less uncertain now. *Phew! Maybe he missed that.*

Anthony half turns, checking himself out from all angles. When he rolls up the sleeves, I catch a flash of something on his left forearm — at first I think it's a bad burn scar. "What is that?" ·

But Anthony has already changed his mind and is rolling the sleeve back down. "It's nothing, it's nothing."

I reach across his chest, grabbing his wrist. "Is that a tattoo? Let me see it."

We're looking at each other — for real — and it's when I see the wide-eyed look of panic in his eyes that I get it. He sighs and says, "Fine," rolling up his sleeve while saying it's dumb, but he doesn't need to say anything. I know what he's going to show me, and I want to tell him it's okay, he doesn't have to — but I can hardly do that now, after making such a show of wanting to see it.

MAYA is written in extravagant lettering on his arm.

"That's your actual *skin*!" I don't mean to sound so shocked, but I can't help it. If he tattooed her name on his body, then clearly his relationship was a little more serious than mine was with Colin! I'd never mistake vandalizing myself for a romantic gesture. I *think*.

"It was just a dumb decision," he says.

"Yours or hers?" The question is out of my mouth before I can stop it. I'm about to apologize, say that was too mean — but if I do, I'd be lying. So, I just let it hang there, even though Anthony looks away all sheepish and embarrassed. There's my answer. "Did she at least get a tattoo of your name?"

"She said she would … when she got home."

I reach out and roll his sleeve back down. Button up his cuff, and stop myself from taking his hand in mine. Instead, I give him a friendly punch on the arm.

"Right, then," I say. "I don't think we're done with Step Two. There's still some making over to get done. Where's the tattoo parlor where you got this?"

Before he can answer, what sounds like the Voice of God — but is really just a manager, I guess — announces that Macy's is closing in … well, I don't hear how many minutes until it closes, because the shoppers on the floor react like their team just lost the Super Series. (I think that's a thing over here.) A groan of annoyance, a gasp of panic — and more than a few curse words.

Anthony has to almost yell to be heard over the mild pandemonium. "Let's pay for the clothes and get out of here, before we get trampled to death."

I nod and start toward the changing rooms, but Anthony's reaching for me, for my collar. Before I know what's happening, he's ripped off the tag to the leather jacket.

I yelp at the snapping sound, even though it's only the jacket that's hurt, not me. "What are you doing?"

"Saving us some time," he says. "Let's just wear these out of the store." The tag for the pants is hanging loose from my waistband; he reaches for it, then freezes, his fingers centimeters away from my thigh …

Looks up at me. "You got that one?"

It takes an effort not to look away, to hold his eyes. I can't do anything about the blushing, though. "Yeah, yeah, I got it, I got it. No worries. I got it."

Nor, it seems, can I do anything about the rambling.

Five minutes later, we're at the front of the line at a checkout, presenting the clerk with a bunch of price tags. The clothes that I wore into the store are still in my tote bag, while Anthony crammed his into his backpack, and when we reach the counter I feel, just for a moment, that I am somehow pushing Colin aside.

Shame I can't cram him in my tote bag for real.

Anthony pays on his credit card, and we leave Macy's, exiting onto Thirty-Fourth Street. Yep, the leather jacket is definitely what I need in this weather. Good job, Anthony — he couldn't tell that his long-distance girlfriend was cheating on him, but he did well here.

"This way," he says, walking east along West Thirty-Fourth.

I follow. "Where are we going?"

"East Village."

✳

6:10 P.M.

We take the N train to Eighth Street–NYU, and Anthony leads me to St. Mark's Place, but I'm not really paying attention because when our train passed Union Square and my mobile beeped, I made the mistake of checking it. There were more Instagram notifications on my lock screen, comments I hadn't noticed while we were in Macy's. My most recently posted photo — a sad selfie with some of the girls from Sacred Heart, on the last day of the semester, when my sadness might not have been as fake as the other girls' — was inundated with sympathy from friends about my missed flight, and I was enjoying the feeling of being more popular than I'd ever been before in my life …

Then I noticed that it was just past six.

Right about now, I should be boarding a plane that *should* be getting ready to take off. Right about now, I *should* be just a few moments away from looking out the window and seeing New York City falling away from me.

But that's not what's happening.

"It's just here." Anthony's voice brings me back to the cold, lonely present, and he leads me down a street that seems to be exclusively for tattoo shops. Now that I'm actually looking at them, I'm less convinced about the big finish to Anthony's makeover. I might be looking a bit tougher than I usually do, but I suspect my cover will be blown when I faint at the sight of a needle!

I'm feeling more and more apprehensive when I start seeing signs for places called Addiction Tattoo (*Please, not that one*) and Whatever

Tattoo (*Who goes into a tattoo parlor all "blah"?*). I'm relieved when Anthony leads me to a place called Love Ink — the name might be a cheesy play on words, but at least the parlor doesn't look like it'll give me hepatitis just from going inside.

"You know, you don't *have* to do this," I tell him. "I was just getting carried away."

He looks at me. "I want to do this."

I believe him, so I let him lead me into the parlor. We walk in, and, like at Macy's, I get slapped in the face by the atmosphere on the other side of the door — except, this time, it's not by the wall of noise from a thousand or more shoppers ...

It's by the stench of pot.

I cough and flap a hand in front of my face, as I let the door close behind me. I take in the parlor, which is not as dingy as I guess I was expecting. It's clean, though the three black reclining chairs look a little like Goth dentist furniture, while the torso art on the walls weirds me out a little. But I have to admit, I'm kind of feeling all the bleeding heart imagery right now. Then I start worrying that, maybe, I've taken this Story down a scary subplot that involves Anthony and me having to escape a psychotic tattoo artist, hell-bent on drawing Satanic images on our backs.

There are no customers inside — just a guy at the counter, staring at a laptop. His skinny, inked-up forearms are folded over his chest (I can't tell if the images are Satanic or not). The laptop screen is turned away from me, but I'd know the dialogue from *It's a Wonderful Life* anywhere.

Anthony clears his throat, and the tattoo artist looks up, squinting like he's trying to find us in the dark. After a second, he turns back to the screen.

Anthony shakes his head. "We're not a hallucination, dude."

The tattoo artist pushes himself off the counter, standing up straight — swaying a bit — and trying to look sober. "What can I do for ya?"

Anthony rolls up his sleeve, revealing the *MAYA* graffiti. "I want to get this covered up."

The tattoo artist peers, leaning forward on the counter. "But, dude, that's *so* great."

"It's fine work," Anthony agrees. "But I still want it covered up."

"That's one of Philomena's, right?" The tattoo artist is literally stroking his chin, like a pompous snob in an art gallery. "I can tell from the way the *y* is swirling, like the letter is actually trying to eat itself. So deep, man ... She'd kill me if she knew I desecrated one of hers."

Anthony looks at me and rolls his eyes, so I step forward and talk to the tattoo artist the way I sometimes have to talk to my friend Heather, after she's had one too many (which is more than once too often).

"My friend's not saying that he doesn't think the tattoo isn't good," I tell him. "Philomena's a true artist. The tattoo is great, but" — I point to Maya's name — "she's not."

He nods, shooting Anthony a sympathetic look. "I got you, man."

"So you can take care of this?" Anthony asks. "Don't you have to, like, tattoo over the original art —"

"Don't worry, don't worry." The guy takes Anthony's arm and leads him to one of the chairs. As Anthony sits down, the guy looks at me. "I know what it's like: new lady in your life, you want to pretend the past never happened. Romantic reboot!"

He laughs for about a minute, and it's only now that I ask myself if Anthony should be getting a tattoo from a guy more baked than the pizza we ate at John's.

"We're not together," Anthony tells him. A little firmly. "I just want the tattoo gone. What can you do about it?"

The guy's stroking his chin again. "You like mermaids?"

✳

6:45 P.M.

Anthony's tattoo is nearly finished. He's looking away from what the tattoo artist — whose name, we found out, is Joe — is doing to his arm. Instead, he's looking at me, and I'm doing my best not to appear totally horrified. Joe's done his best — and at a pace I was not expecting from a bloke as high as a lost kite — but the mermaid tail that he made from Maya's name is wide and shapeless and the scales he attempted look more like stars. He's drawn her arms in what I *think* is supposed to be a graceful, floaty pose but instead makes her look like she's giving jazz hands. And the face ... let's just say, she's got a face on her like she's just been electrocuted. This must be Joe's first attempt at a mermaid.

But it was *his* idea!

About five minutes ago, Anthony asked me, through gritted teeth, "How's it looking?" I answered with a big nod rather than words, because I didn't trust my voice not to sound as freaked out as I was feeling. I was also kind of hoping that Joe was going somewhere with the design — that, at the very end, it was all going to come together into something wonderful that would surprise me. But nope — it started terrible and remained terrible. And by the time I realized it was going to stay terrible, it was too late.

Maybe, a few months from now, Anthony can go to a different tattoo parlor and get the whole thing totally blacked out. A perfect black rectangle — ooh, maybe with a doorknob, symbolizing that he's *closed the door* on what's her name!

"All righty, there you go, man." Joe puts his needle on the stainless steel side table (with admirable care for a guy who still looks like he thinks all of this is just a dream), then leans back in his chair, admiring his own work. "That, if I say so myself, is really, really cool."

Anthony sits up. I'm trying really hard not to cringe and to grin as encouragingly as I can, but I can feel from the tightness of my cheek muscles that, at best, I'm offering him a *gringe*.

He winces, looks down. Takes in the lopsided, electrocuted mermaid doing jazz hands. Holds his arm right up to his face, his lips twitching, and I instinctively look toward Joe's tools, hoping that Anthony doesn't reach for them. I brace myself for him to lose it, go full-on Brooklyn — whatever that is, I wouldn't know — maybe pick up the needle himself and forcibly tattoo Joe in revenge. But he doesn't do that. Instead, he sits calmly while Joe bandages him up, pays what the tattoo costs, says thanks and guides me out of the parlor and back onto St. Mark's.

He doesn't actually *like* the tattoo, does he?

✳

Five minutes later, we're in a diner farther along St. Mark's. We walked past at least five more tattoo places on the way here, and each time we passed one, I wondered if Anthony was thinking the same thing I was — that, maybe, we should have gone somewhere else to de-Maya his arm.

Now, we're sitting opposite each other, a plate of cheese fries on the table between us. I didn't think I'd be hungry so soon after that pizza, but the fries taste *amazing*. Maybe inhaling all that pot smoke gave me the munchies. I glance at Anthony's arm, and I have to ask, because I can't take it any longer. "Are you ... okay with that?"

Anthony looks down at the bandage. It feels almost like the abomination underneath is shining through.

He shrugs. "It's just my arm," he says, before shoveling a cheese fry into his mouth.

I stare at him, trying to figure out if he's joking. But he can't be joking — he looks dead serious ...

… but then I remember one of the things that my semester here taught me about Americans — that, despite what some Brits still insist, Americans *can* do dry humor, irony and sarcasm. The idea that they can't is as wrong as the stereotype of the British "stiff upper lip." If *that* were true, I wouldn't have done all the crying I've done since Colin said he "just didn't," and I certainly wouldn't be leaning facedown on the table, literally cackling, like I am right now.

Soon, I've laughed so much, I feel like I'm about to vomit. I look up at Anthony, wiping tears from my eyes. "I'm really sorry. I shouldn't have dragged you —"

"Don't sweat it," he says, rolling his sleeve down, smiling and shaking his head — I guess at himself. "I mean, however I covered it up, I was going to have to live with it. It's not *gone*. Just … hidden." He falls quiet then, his smile fading. "Seems kind of fitting."

"What does?"

"This … Her name, her mark, it's always going to be there. Like, you can't see it now, obviously, but the mark made on my skin hasn't been taken *away*."

"There's no laser removal for love." No gringe this time — this time, I full on cringe, because that was totally lame.

But Anthony's not rolling his eyes or scoffing at me. Instead, he's nodding. "Right. I can act like it's not there, but it is — just like I can pretend I was never with Maya at all, but I was."

"Or," I say, "you could hope to get a really bad concussion one day. Knock all those memories right out of your head."

He just smiles at me. "If I still played football, maybe I'd have a chance at that. But I gave it up, sophomore year." Then he looks down at the table, and I almost don't catch the next part: "My dad *really* approved of that decision."

He looks back up at me, so suddenly that I start. "What do you want to do after this?"

I just look at him blankly — if I'm being honest, I'm starting to feel a bit tired. But he's got something in his eyes — an eagerness I've not seen until now.

I'm totally out of ideas, except for one: I take the tote bag out from under the table. "Shall we have a look at Step Three?" I ask.

When I see what Step Three is, I frown. This one's not going to be easy ...

2. ~~EXPLORE ALTERNATIVE YOUS~~ ...

~ CHAPTER FOUR ~

ANTHONY

3. RECONNECT WITH AN OLD FRIEND ...

None of us like to admit it, but the first thing to change about us when we go from Single to Coupled is that we lose contact with old friends. But by letting friends fall away, are we not letting parts of our old self — our original, true self — fall away, too? Sometimes, to create the new, better You, you must first remember what you loved about the Old You.

7:00 P.M.

Charlotte turns the book around so that I can see the page.

The third chapter title says, "Reconnect with an old friend." I catch a glimpse of text that explains how "old friends" are a good way of reminding you of your "old self" — I guess, your prerelationship self — before Charlotte puts the book down.

"Well, that sucks," I say. "I'm guessing all your old friends are back home."

Charlotte nods. "And it's midnight there, so Skyping is out. Of course, if I had any of my old friends' Skype details, they wouldn't be old friends — they'd be new friends. Well, not new, but ... present, you know?"

Then she does this cute little thing I've seen her do every time she's rambled tonight. She catches herself, closes her eyes, wrinkles her nose like she's giving herself a silent command not to ramble. I want to tell her not to bother — I like the rambling. Everything Maya said always felt planned, rehearsed somehow. This feels more honest. Then I tell myself that, after what happened today, it's probably a good idea for me to sit on the bench for a while. She's going back to England, anyway, so it's not like anything real could happen ...

"But *you* could look up an old friend," she suggests, stuffing the book back into her bag. She's not even bothering — *we're* not even bothering — to read the full chapter explaining *why* we should reconnect with old friends; just like we didn't read up on why we should do something we'd stopped doing or what a makeover was really going to do for us.

I'm not all that keen on reaching out to any of *my* old friends, but Charlotte is staring at me with what looks like hope, and I'm still cool with anything that keeps me from going home — and, for some reason, I'm also feeling like I really, really don't want to let her down. So I take out my phone and warn her, "You asked for it. I think these guys will be a totally different kind of American from what you're used to."

"As long as they're not hipsters, I'm sure I'll get along with them just fine."

I shrug. "For all I know, they could be hipsters now. *Old* friends, remember?"

I look down at my phone, thumb hovering over the WhatsApp icon in the top left corner of the screen — ignoring the badge over the Snapchat icon that tells me I have seven notifications. I should really change the settings so that I *don't* get told every single thing that Maya's doing anymore — that wasn't okay even when we *were* together. I open up WhatsApp, where there's a group chat for my senior class. It hasn't had a new message posted since before the end of the summer. Probably everyone on it is wrapped up in college, and no one checks it anymore, but Charlotte doesn't have to know that — she only needs to know that I tried. I send a two-line message about being in the city, if anyone's around. I close the app and stare at my home screen for a second, willing myself not to go onto Snapchat — even if that damned red badge is now saying "8," and finding out what eight noteworthy things could possibly have happened to Maya in the last forty-five minutes or so feels like something I should absolutely do.

I stuff the phone in my pants pocket, look at Charlotte. "Want to get out of here?"

＊

Ten minutes later, we're passing the Washington Square Arch, walking for the sake of walking, neither one of us sure who's in the lead. I guess it's me, since I actually live here.

Bleecker was strangely dead earlier, but this part of the village isn't. Tourists are gathered at the arch, and locals are barging through them with hands in their pockets, heads angled down and shoulders hunched against the snow that's settling on the sidewalks. Unlike me, some people just *want* to get home tonight.

Charlotte stops, looks at the arch. I really, really hope she's not going to ask me to take a photo of her or, worse, take a selfie — but she doesn't seem like a selfie kind of girl. I like that.

"Penny for your thoughts," I ask, because I literally can't think of anything else.

She smiles at me. "Shouldn't you guys say, 'A cent for your thoughts'?"

I make a face. "Yeah, because that has *such* a ring to it."

She looks back to the arch, still smiling, thinking. "A cent for ... your *sense* ... of ... No, you're right. Penny's better." The smile eases off her face. "I was just people-watching."

"You like to do that?"

She nods. "Why? Is that weird?"

I shrug, tell her: "I'm kind of the same. What caught your eye?"

She shrugs back. "Nothing in particular. Just ... these are people who all *planned* to be here at Christmas. Most of them probably live here, but some have got to be far from home, right? But I guess, since they're with people they know and love, they don't *feel* all that far away from home. You know what I mean?"

I look down at my feet. "I've never really been out of New York."

"Seriously?" She laughs. I make a face that says, *I know, isn't it terrible?* "Well," she goes on, "I'm starting to think it's the not knowing anybody here that makes me feel the distance, more than the actual distance. I don't know if I'm making sense at all" — she kind of is, kind of isn't — "but it's got me thinking about the idea of 'home.' The whole time I was here, studying, I was telling myself that I was making New York my home, just by being here ... that it would be the same when — if — I came back to study at Columbia. But now I realize, I was wrong — at least a little bit. Without my host family and their house as a base, everyone's a stranger."

"There'll be school next year," I tell her. "That's pretty good as a base. And people won't stay strangers on campus for very long."

She nods, adjusts the tote bag on her shoulder, then folds her arms over her chest. She stays silent a long time, but not the kind of silent a person gets when they've got nothing to say. She's silent because she's thinking.

And it feels very important to me that I don't interrupt her.

"I guess it's just annoying," she says to the sidewalk, "to have in your head the idea that you're going to have this great semester, and you're going to truly find yourself — answer all of the questions you have about who you'll be in the future, what you're capable of … and when it comes down to it, and you have to decide what to do, you start to feel like you just want to go home. And you know what the worst part is? I am actually starting to feel angry at my family because *I'm* missing them. Is that messed up?"

"Oh, totally," I tell her, as an old couple walk past us, arm in arm. I hate myself for wondering, is this their last Christmas together? "But you know what? Home is home. It's always going to be 'where you're from' — you can't change that. You're thinking of it as a physical base, a place where everything always beg*ins*. Maybe the trick is to think of it as an emotional base, where everything beg*an*. Life's a journey, but you sound like you're preparing to run laps around a single track, when you should be, like … I dunno, running a marathon."

She's not looking at the sidewalk anymore. She's looking at me, with an expression I can't read. Her eyes are narrowed, and her lips are pursed, smoothing out her cheek dimples a little.

"You think it's better to move forward?" she asks.

I snap my fingers, point at her — suddenly wanting to change this conversation to a lighthearted one. "That's exactly it. Move forward. Thank you for translating my long-winded ramble into a single sentence."

She smiles, looks back at the park behind the arch. Thinks it over.

"So, anyway," I say, "about Step Three. You seriously don't know anybody in New York? Besides me, obviously. Didn't you just spend a whole semester at a high school? Surely you made some friends."

"Oh, yeah, I did …" She stuffs her hands into her pockets, hunches her shoulders against the cold, shuffles from foot to foot. "Well, not *friends* friends, but there were girls I used to sit with at lunch and stuff."

I lean down, find her eyes. "And let me guess — Colin came along and things changed?" She nods. "Well, I guess those girls at lunch count as honorary old friends for you. They're the closest you've got here."

"You think I should message them?"

I think she totally should. Because her new old friends have got to be a better option than anyone from my senior class who might answer my lame WhatsApp message.

But I try not to look too eager when I say: "Why not?"

She shrugs, takes out her phone and sends a group message on her own WhatsApp. She puts her phone back in her inside jacket pocket when she's done, then turns to look at me, and we're left looking awkwardly at each other because, for the first time in the three hours or so that we've known each other, we have nothing more to say.

I ought to be used to this, because it happened with Maya — a lot. It's only now that I think maybe that was a clear sign we weren't right for each other.

Or maybe I'm just bad at talking to girls.

But I'm not panicking with Charlotte the way I'd panic when this happened with Maya. The silence is kind of awkward, but it doesn't feel like it matters — she's leaving soon and will probably forget me before she's finished her first cup of tea back home.

When she says, "So ..." I know she's feeling as awkward as I am, and the Thing to Say just sort of comes to me.

"What do *you* feel like doing?" She looks at me as if she doesn't understand the question. "I mean, we should do something. Anything. These are your last few hours in the city. We can't just stand around waiting for our phones to ping." (If and when my phone pings, it's not going to be who I want it to be anyway.)

She stares at the sidewalk, her smile punching the dimples back into her cheeks. Why do I keep noticing them?

"Well, I suppose there *is* something …" She's looking nervous about asking. *Oh, man, she's going to ask me to take her to the Empire State Building. I just know it.* "But it's kind of lame."

Yep, she's going to ask to go to the Empire State Building.

She looks at me, half embarrassed and half teasing. Whatever it is, it's not going to be good. "It's typical and obvious and all of that stuff, but … I don't know, this might be my last day here, so it *would* be kind of fun …"

✳

Next thing I know, I'm at the West Fourth Street–Washington Square station, en route to, of all places, the Empire State Building. Charlotte's walking straight for the stairs, but I reach out to take a handful of sleeve and pull her back. I point at the IFC across the street. "How about we catch a movie?" I ask her, hearing the desperation in my own voice.

She turns around, gives me this grin that says she's not having any of it. "I'm a visitor here. You should *want* to show off your city."

"You don't understand. Christmas Eve, everyone gets the same lame idea that they have to have a perfect kiss on top of the Empire State Building, in the snow." I may or may not be talking about the plans I had for tonight, before the Airport Incident. "We're gonna be standing in line until New Year's."

We sidestep to make way for a middle-aged couple coming out of the station. They are wearing matching beige trench coats and walking side by side — in perfect step and perfect silence, the kind of married couple who have been in love for so long they probably gave up on PDAs in the nineties.

"I've been here almost four months," Charlotte says, "and I've spent most of my time inside a classroom or in the Lawrences' house, studying. I haven't seen the Statue of Liberty, the Rockefeller Center or the UN. I should at least cross something lame and obvious off the list, right?"

I can't really argue with that, but I also can't pretend like I'm down for this — I'm actually taking out my phone and hoping that some random, forgotten high school buddy has responded to my WhatsApp message. But my lock screen shows no notifications. Just my background image — the selfie that Maya made me take in the airport on the day she left for college. I'm kissing her cheek, and she's looking off camera, like something — some*one* — has caught her eye. Of course she is.

"It's not like you have anything better to do," Charlotte says. Her voice is teasing, but, for a moment, it reminds me a little too much of the condescending tone that Maya would use sometimes, the Maya who apparently couldn't give me her full attention even when I was kissing her goodbye, and I can hear in my own voice that I'm kind of snapping at Charlotte more than I should be.

"It's Christmas Eve. Of *course* no one's checking their phone every five minutes."

She sighs, like she's annoyed — just irritated. Maya would have gasped and looked like she was about to cry. "Yes or no," she says, half turning to point to the subway station. "Yes or no, can we get a train from this station to the Empire State Building?"

I don't answer, but she can see from my face that we can — F train, D train. We can be there in ten minutes.

"Right, then, since we just happened to be walking this way — for no reason, let's be honest — I say we call this fate. Let's go."

I really should have taken charge when we left the diner.

Charlotte leads me into the station but stops at the bottom of the stairs. Sitting there is a bedraggled, balding guy in a tatty parka, a cardboard sign in front of him asking for five bucks for dog food, an arrow pointing to the sleeping puppy — a white English bulldog — nestled in the crook of his arm. He sees us see him (well, he sees us see the dog) and starts stroking its head.

"You guys got it in your hearts to help me feed this girl?"

I really don't want to play the cynical New Yorker in front of Charlotte, but I don't buy it. I roll my eyes when she drops into a crouch to join the guy in petting the dog, who is just starting to wake up.

"What's her name?" Charlotte asks.

I'm trying to figure out how to pull her away, so she doesn't get lured into some kind of scam — but before I can do anything, my phone buzzes against my leg, and my chest clenches with what could be dread but is probably hope. Maybe it's Maya. Maybe she's gotten tired of Handsome Hipster already and is thinking she's made a huge mistake.

I take my phone out and see that I've got not a text but a WhatsApp message — it *might* still be from Maya — but when I go in to see it, I just get a white screen with the gray ring of doom, like the app's saying, "Damn, I know the message is here somewhere, Anthony. I just had it. But God knows what I did with it. I'm such a dumbass." The signal's not strong enough down here.

Charlotte's still petting the puppy, who's wide awake now and licking her hand. The guy in the parka says something about not wanting to take her to a shelter, and I know I should start hustling Charlotte down to the tracks, even if she does want to do something lame and touristy like go to the Empire State Building, but ...

What if it's Maya, saying she's kicked Handsome Hipster to the curb, and that she really does want me to spend Christmas with her family after all?

I know this is a terrible idea. And I hate myself for wanting it to be Maya. But I also know that there's no way I'm *not* going to look at the message. So, while Charlotte is cooing over the dog, I lean down, tell her I'll be right back, then take the steps two at a time back up to street level.

The WhatsApp message isn't from Maya. It's from someone named Vinnie Zampanti, who says that he's going caroling with his choir group in the East Village in twenty minutes, and I'm totally welcome to join if I want, and it doesn't matter if I'm not a singer.

Who the heck is Vinnie Zampanti? He responded to the group message I sent, so he must be an old classmate, but the name is not ringing any bells at all. I click on his name, go to his profile — but his picture is just a wedge of Gouda cheese (not exactly a good sign).

Seriously, who's Vinnie? And why would he think anyone would randomly want to go caroling in the East Village on Christmas Eve? Then I think, maybe I can sell this to Charlotte as a *real* New York experience — local flavor, something like that. Anything that keeps me off the top of the Empire State Building tonight. So I type thanks to Vinnie and add that I'll try to swing by, then turn around to go get Charlotte.

But I don't have to go get her — she's already at the top of the stairs.

Walking an English bulldog puppy.

"Oh, you gotta be kidding me!" I'm pinching the bridge of my nose like I have a splitting headache, which is something all Monteleone men do when we're stressed out. Luke copied Dad, and I copied Luke — and then Dad told me not to imitate my big brother all the time, that I should be my own man. I was seven.

"I could tell that guy down there wasn't after money for dog food," she says, handing me the puppy's leash — as if I want it. "He was conning commuters, obviously — I could actually see an iPhone in his pocket. It looked newer than mine!"

"So you took ..."

"Bought."

"Oh, man ..."

"Fifty dollars." She's beaming at me like she's gotten the best deal in the world. "Small price to pay to save a dog from an owner who, I can tell, didn't care about her. She can go to a better home. A loving home."

"Where? In England? You want to take the puppy with you? You're getting on a plane in a few hours, and there are rules about this kind of thing. Quarantines, paperwork — I don't even know!"

She's shaking her head at me. "We've got all night." She kneels down to fuss over the puppy, who squirms and yaps, and, despite myself, I feel an insistent urge to pick her up. "Who wouldn't want to take this little princess home with them? It'll be fine. Also ..." She takes out her book. The book that's gotten me into this mess. It's only now I notice that there's a puppy on the damned cover.

"I think I remember something ..." She flicks through the pages. "Yes! I thought I remembered seeing this chapter. Look — Step Four." She turns the book around and shows it to me: "'Take care of somebody else — so that you remember how to take care of You.'"

"So, what? We're doing the whole book now?"

She looks at me over the top of the puppy's head. "Why not? It's worked well for us so far, right? All the experiences we've had — I wanted a Story, and I'm definitely getting one. Plus" — she holds up the dog to make her point — "we're taking steps by accident — maybe this is meant to be or something."

"Okay, slow down" — the dog chooses this moment to start licking my boots; kinda gross, but Charlotte thinks it's hilarious — "we didn't even do Step Three yet."

"I don't think the book said we had to do them in an exact sequence."

How would you know? I wonder, as she puts the book back in her bag, unread. *You've barely skimmed the surface of that book. For all you know, Step Eight could tell you to walk backward across Times Square with your eyes closed.*

"Do you even know anything about dogs?" I ask her.

"Oh, yeah," she says. "We have a Staffie called Rocky, and there's no way this little lady could ever give me as many problems as he does. Now, she needs a name!" Charlotte kisses the dog's head. "I was thinking 'Winny,' because she looks a little bit like Winston Churchill — but that's too obvious. Plus, people might hear it and think she's named after Pooh Bear."

She looks back at me, beaming in exactly the same way she did when she told me she paid "only" fifty bucks for the dog. But I can tell that the eagerness in her eyes isn't just about taking care of the dog. Some things are making sense to me now. The impulsiveness, the rambling — she's using anything she can to not think about her ex. Like, if she just keeps moving, keeps talking — if she doesn't slow down — she won't have time or brain space to think about him. She's running from *her* breakup. I'm trying to run *after* mine.

And here we both are, in the same exact place.

4. *TAKE CARE OF SOMEBODY ELSE — SO THAT YOU REMEMBER HOW TO TAKE CARE OF YOU.*

It's hard to think about how to take care of yourself, isn't it? A lot of us convince ourselves that we're Just Fine, that we don't need looking after. Breakups can show us that, yes, we do need looking after — and when we suddenly start needing to be looked after, we often feel like there's no one around to look after us. And, oftentimes, our heads are so compromised by the emotional tsunamis raging through them that we just don't know what we want — or what we need. At times like this, it can be good to find someone who needs You more than You need someone else ...

✳

About fifteen minutes later, I'm carrying the dog, who seems to really like the taste of my face, to the Starbucks at Second Avenue and Ninth Street. Along the way, Charlotte ponders Winny's new name. I suggest "Mistake" — a joke I instantly regret, because neither one of us seems all that ready to laugh about stuff. But Charlotte actually likes it.

"Do you see him?" she asks.

We're looking for this "Vinnie" guy — though it's not like I'd recognize him if my life depended on it. But Charlotte's eyes lit up at the mention of caroling, and I'm pretty sure mine lit up when I realized I wouldn't have to endure the Empire State Building tonight, so here we are.

I look down Ninth Street and see that there's a group of people standing in a shivering huddle outside the coffee shop. Do they look like carolers? I have no idea. Just like I have no idea if one of them is the mysterious Vinnie. I can't admit to Charlotte I have no idea who I'm looking for, because I've already kind of made out that Vinnie's a good buddy — why did I do that? — so I'm acting like I can't quite see through all the winter coats and beanie hats on the folks in this crowd. As we get closer, I realize that Charlotte and I are going to bring down the average age of this group by about twenty-two years. I slow to a stop about ten feet from them, Mistake trying to wriggle free from my arms to run over to the new people I'm not sure about caroling with when, thank God, I recognize somebody — just not somebody I expected to see among carolers.

"What's up, Cheese?" I call to the short, ferret-faced guy wriggling free from the pack, almost losing his Santa hat in the process. The accordion tucked under his arm gasps a few off-key notes as he walks toward us.

"That can't be his name," Charlotte mumbles.

"No," I mumble back, realizing that I'd either forgotten or never knew that Cheese's actual name was Vinnie Zampanti. He transferred to a new school between junior and senior year. By rights, he shouldn't even be on that WhatsApp group chat. "We just called him that 'cause he was addicted to Gouda."

"Ant, you made it!"

And now Cheese — Vinnie — is hugging me, almost dropping his accordion, and it's like my brain is unlocking memories. I remember that Vinnie Zampanti was kind of the weird kid in class and called me "Ant" ever since we were in Cub Scouts together. I've hated the nickname since Cub Scouts. "Good to see you, dude."

"Yeah, yeah," I say, trying not to look distracted by the memory of my cousin Marie telling me that, in eighth grade, Cheese attempted to serenade her with his rendition of … well, Marie could never figure out what he was singing, because she could barely hear him over the accordion. *If I'd known it was Cheese who answered that WhatsApp message …*

"Okay, people, let's move out." One of the women in the group — in her fifties, short, stout, all authority — takes a step toward the curb, gathering people to her. "We will start along Ninth Street, heading west. Hope you've all got your song sheets, and that you all remember your — who are you?"

She's looking at me and Charlotte.

"No, no, it's cool, Gladys." Cheese claps me on the shoulder, so hard I almost drop Mistake, who barks her annoyance. "This here's a childhood buddy of mine. One of the best singers I know."

I'm starting to think Cheese might have me mixed up with some other "Ant." I don't sing. But Gladys is asking Cheese what my range is, and Cheese is insisting I sing bass and Charlotte sings something called mezzo-soprano. Gladys seems happy to hear this and leads the group past us, along Ninth Street, saying that this is a relief, because they didn't have a bass or a mezzo.

I let the group get some distance before I follow. I turn to Cheese, who's standing on my left. Charlotte's on my right. "What was that about?"

Cheese just grins at me. He looks so much like a ferret, it's kind of disturbing. "Don't worry about it. Just stand at the back and lip-sync it." And then he's throwing his free arm around me like we're old buddies. Mistake gives him a couple of sniffs, then turns her head away. Guess we're never feeding her cheese. "It's good to see you, man. But I gotta be honest, I, erm …" He flicks a glance past me, at Charlotte. "I'm a little disappointed you brought your new girl."

I'm about to ask why, but Charlotte gets in first. "Actually, I'm just here because my flight home was canceled."

Every time Cheese smiles, I regret more and more coming here — sending that group message in the first place. "What are you doing in a choir, anyway? It looks like it's just old ladies, soccer moms and you." I do a quick scan. "You're the only guy here."

"Exactly." Cheese is not only smiling his ferret smile, he's nodding in slow motion. "It's genius, man. I'm the willing elk walking suicidally into the pride."

Charlotte makes a sound of general disgust. "What does *that* mean?"

"You know, cougars," says Cheese. "I'm a big piece of prey that's just begging to be eaten alive."

Up ahead, the group is beginning to cross First Avenue, and one of the women — who looks older than my mom — turns and makes a kissy face at Cheese. He blows a kiss back at her, and I beg my brain not to imagine what might happen after we're done here. We cross First Avenue, and Gladys brings us to a stop outside the first house that we come to. She commands someone to ring the doorbell, and when an old guy in a red-and-black sweater opens the door, she turns to face us, pointing at Cheese to make sure he's ready. Then she raises her arms, preparing to count us off into who-knows-what carol. No one's given us a song sheet!

What child is this, who, laid to rest,
On Mary's lap is sleeping?

Oh, I know this one. I think. We used to sing it in middle school. I vaguely move my lips in time to the melody, so that it *looks* like I'm singing, and hope that the words will come to me, but they don't. I know there's a "Christ" and a few more "Marys" in there somewhere. I think shepherds might be mentioned, as well.

I turn to Charlotte, who's singing (she sounds quite good, actually) while looking at me, like, *Seriously?* Come on, it's not like I don't know the words to the national anthem.

I know that "the babe, the son of Mary" is the end of the first verse, so while the singers take a breath, and Cheese harasses this stretch of Ninth Street with an accordion solo that is surely not in the classic version, I try again to remember what comes next. But then I think, screw it, I'll make up my own lyrics and trust that I'll be drowned out by everyone else:

What child is this, I don't know this kid,
I didn't order no child ...

I would totally have gotten away with it, if everyone else had been singing. But I was going off what I remembered of the melody, and not Gladys's conducting — big mistake, because Cheese was still soloing — so it's just me and my not-bass voice ruining a Christmas standard. Mistake wriggles in my arms and howls — in harmony or protest, I'm not quite sure — and even Cheese stops playing to gawk at me.

I feel like both an idiot and an asshole, until Charlotte snorts and hides her face in the scarf I bought her.

Somehow, that makes this whole embarrassing situation okay.

Gladys turns and apologizes to the old dude at the door. "We're breaking in some new singers," she says, then glares at me and Charlotte. "They have a *lot* to learn."

The old dude goes back inside and closes the door, and the Cougar Choir heads down the steps to circle me and Charlotte. As they start yelling at us — one of them even says we've "ruined Christmas" — I hear the hiss and whine of Cheese's accordion as he puts himself between us and them.

"Hey, hey, hey, beauties, beauties!" He's patting the air as if telling them to sit down. "Relax, don't get upset. These two are friends of mine. They didn't mean anything by that — they just really, really wanted to join in on the fun, that's all. They're sorry." He looks at me, and with his face turned away from the group, he lets his real motive show.

Dude, don't blow this for me.

"Right, Ant?"

"Yeah, sure," I say, shifting Mistake from one arm to the other. She's getting heavy. "I guess I just had too much Christmas spirit. I'm really sorry."

Gladys doesn't look any happier, but she does give a nod. "Apology accepted. But this is a *semiprofessional choir*, and we can't let just anyone join. We have to have standards."

Charlotte scoffs. "Where's *your* Christmas spirit?"

"Okay," I say, grabbing Charlotte's hand and starting to tug her back down Ninth Street. "We're done here. Let's go."

Charlotte walks with me, while Mistake leans across my chest and shoulder, trying to nibble at her hair. "Guess we're not going to be starting our own choir anytime soon."

Behind me, I hear some of the carolers groan as Cheese tells them that he'll catch up when they're on Tenth Street, he's just going to grab a coffee with his friends.

Oh, shit — he means us.

✳

And this is how I find myself in some place called Evening Joe's, having coffee with Cheese. The staff wasn't sure about letting us in with

Mistake, but Charlotte told them the whole story of her day, and I don't know if it was her tale of woe or the fact that she told it in a British accent — that I swear veered more toward *Downton Abbey* than at any other time today — but they relented and just asked us to make sure the pup didn't run wild. Or pee anywhere.

"Don't worry about Gladys …" Cheese lifts his coffee and takes a big, loud slurp, letting the cup clatter back on the table. It becomes very annoying, very quickly.

Step Three kind of sucks.

"She just likes to be in control." Then he does this thing with his eyebrows — wiggles one, then the other, making them wriggle like caterpillars doing the worm — that reminds me why I never became friends with him in high school. "Trust me."

Charlotte's holding Mistake and doing a good job of looking like she's not trying to un-see Cheese's eyebrows. "What exactly *is* a semiprofessional choir?"

Cheese admits that he's not sure. "One time, we got fifty bucks for singing at a nursing home." I try not to laugh — but thankfully, Cheese moves the conversation away from the carolers. He tells me that he's taking a break from Fordham. "You still at Columbia?" I nod. "Majoring in English, right?" I nod again.

Charlotte looks surprised — maybe even shocked. "You didn't tell me you go to Columbia," she says.

I shrug. "Well, it never came up."

She holds my eye for a long, long second, and I start wishing that I could tell what she's thinking. We'll be going to the same school, if she comes back. Does she think that's a good thing or a bad thing?

Do *I* think it's a good thing or a bad thing?

Charlotte hands Mistake to me, saying that she'll be right back, and gets up to go to the bathroom.

Cheese watches her go, then turns back to me with a face that says,

Not bad. "I gotta say, though, bro, I was a little disappointed to see you show up without your last girlfriend. She was *fine.*"

I think back to junior year, the last time Cheese and I were sort of classmates. I didn't have a girlfriend junior year, except ... "Wait, are you talking about Tammy? We went to, like, two movies."

"No, man" — *slurp, slurp, clang* — "the blonde. What's her name? Maya."

I stare at him. *Wait a minute.* "How do you know I dated Maya?"

"She was all over your Instagram, bro. Every new photo was a selfie with that girl."

I need to set my Instagram to private.

Cheese isn't done. "I'm just sorry you didn't post any beach shots or, like, underwear stuff. You totally failed your boys there, man. Also, what the hell were you thinking, letting her get away? What are you, some kind of idiot or something? I mean, she wasn't just out of your league — you were like ... a Triple A player the Mets were just letting hang around and wear their jersey — even letting you get on the field sometimes."

Mistake whines and burrows into the crook of my arm, like she can sense the anger that's rising inside of me. I stare at the table, listening to the *slurp, slurp* of Cheese drinking his coffee. Step Three on a mission to forget about Maya has led me to a cougar-chasing asshole who wants to talk about nothing but her — and I wonder, am I so angry because Cheese kind of nailed it? That I spent a lot of the time I was with Maya — if our weird, bicoastal setup could be called being "with" each other — trying to convince myself to believe my "luck"?

I drain what's left of my coffee. I'm not sticking around. Charlotte's coming back from the bathroom, and when she sees the look on my face, she breaks stride. I lightly shake my head at her — *I'm fine, but we're out of here.*

I call for the check and pretty much pretend Cheese isn't there, isn't talking to me, isn't asking for Maya's number. I pay for everything, even his coffee, hand Charlotte her tote bag and hook my backpack over my shoulder.

"Get back to granny-grabbing, Cheese."

"Was it something I said?" he asks, making to stand up. I put a hand on his shoulder to stop him, and he sits back down. He might be an idiot, but he can at least sense that I'm mad at him. I turn around, handing Mistake's leash to Charlotte, and we walk out, back onto Ninth Street, heading toward Second Avenue.

"What was all that about?" she asks.

"Just me learning that some people need to be let go," I tell her.

We stop on the corner at Second. Charlotte's suddenly distracted by Mistake, who's wriggling like she wants to escape.

"Oh, dear, I think little madam here needs a wee."

I try to warn Charlotte we could get a hundred-dollar fine if Mistake has other, grosser ideas. We cross Second Avenue, and take Mistake over to a tree, where she goes number one — thankfully, just that — in the dirt.

As I tune out the sound of Charlotte encouraging and then congratulating the pup, I start to feel sick — and not just from the stench that's rising up from the dirt. Cheese is an odd dude — a full-on weirdo — but despite everything, I find myself feeling like I agree with him: I was an idiot to let Maya get away.

But you didn't. She ran. *And she did it on Christmas Eve, of all days. That makes it even worse ... You're better off without her.*

I really, really wish I could agree with the thought.

"Okay." Charlotte walks Mistake back down Ninth Street again.

I nudge her arm. "Hey, does this mean we've crossed off Step Four now? I mean, we did rescue her from the subway station and got her through peeing. I think that counts as taking care of her, right?"

She beams at me the same way she did when she first got Mistake. When *we* first got her. "Yeah, let's cross it off."

I return her smile, and, for just a second, our arms nudge against each other, and we feel like something more than two strangers killing time in New York.

Then Charlotte's phone buzzes, and she jumps away from me in surprise. She apologizes and takes it out of her tote bag. Makes a face that is half surprised and half apprehensive. "It's this girl Katie, answering that message I sent earlier," she says. "I know her from school. She says she's throwing a party at her cousin's apartment in the city tonight and says it's totally fine if we want to go."

She's looking at me, trying to gauge what I think. A high school party isn't something I really want to go to, but I also don't want to disappoint her (I already failed to take her to the Empire State Building). So, I point to the tote bag. "Can we make a step out of it?"

Charlotte takes out the book, flicks through it front to back. Then back to front. Stops at a chapter in the middle. Step Six. We're skipping Five, for now.

"'Go twenty-four hours without mentioning your ex.'" She looks up at me and shrugs. "Well, I'm not going to even be here that long, so ... maybe we could just try it at the party, and see how we get on?"

It's looking like I'm not getting out of this party. As much as I want to do anything else — even biting the bullet and going home, telling my family what happened and getting it over with seems preferable — I also feel a need to keep an eye on Charlotte. And Mistake's licking my boots again (Christ, what am I going to do with this dog?).

When I answer her, I realize it was never in doubt.

"Where is this party?"

3. RECONNECT WITH AN OLD FRIEND ...

4. TAKE CARE OF SOMEBODY ELSE — SO THAT YOU REMEMBER HOW TO TAKE CARE OF YOU.

~ CHAPTER FIVE ~

CHARLOTTE

6. *GO TWENTY-FOUR HOURS WITHOUT*
MENTIONING YOUR EX.

We all know that words have power — but names *have even greater power. To create distance between yourself and your ex, you must take away that power. And the only way to do that is through silence.*

8:30 P.M.

"Hey, I was only six!"

I blush at the way Anthony covers his mouth to stifle his laughter. I've just confessed that I called my first cat Hagrid, because I was huge into Harry Potter — plus, the cat was big and fat and fluffy, so of course any six-year-old would think of Hagrid!

"Everyone named their pets for Harry Potter characters back then," I mumble as the 1 train that we're on pulls into Fourteenth Street station. Three people get on our car, including yet one more

Williamsburgy type in a black cardigan. Not knowing any better, he sits opposite Mistake, who wriggles in my arms and growls — the pup *really* has it in for hipsters!

I stroke Mistake's head and whisper at her to calm down. She does. Beside me, Anthony reaches over and scratches behind her ear. "You're good at settling her," he says.

"I have some experience soothing pooches," I tell him. "My dog, Rocky, kind of hates all men. Except my dad."

"You serious?"

I nod. "It's a real problem. We walk him in this park near our house, but first my sister Jessica has to do a recon to make sure there are no guys. Maybe he's allergic to Y chromosomes."

"Maybe he just mistrusts anyone not family? Like he sees them as people who might want to *join* you guys, you know? Competition."

I don't answer Anthony because the only thing I can think to say is that I kind of want to bring Colin home to London, so that I can sic Rocky on him. And if I said that, then I would have failed at our revised, shortened Step Six — having proper conversations without mentioning our exes until we've left Katie's party, which is where we're headed right now.

Anthony suggested we give it a trial run, and he went first and couldn't think of anything for a bit, but then Mistake licked my face, making me laugh, and he asked me about pets I'd had in the past. It wasn't exactly brilliant conversation, but it got us started ...

Until I ended up thinking about *him* anyway. And even though I wasn't mentioning him, I was constantly thinking about not mentioning him, which meant that he was on my mind, and I don't know if that defeated the purpose or not.

It's now my turn to get Anthony started. We've got about ten or eleven stops left until we reach 116th Street, our stop. I ask him what his favorite sport is, because he's a guy and I expect he'll have an answer — but he says he doesn't really like sports at all anymore (I'm kind of pleased to hear this). I ask about his favorite movies, and he totally doesn't surprise me by saying *Inception*. But I've got nothing after that. And we've passed only Fiftieth Street. We both stare at our shoes, having finally run out of things to say to each other. Just as I'm consoling myself that we had a good run, Anthony pulls something out of the air.

"You believe in parallel realities?"

He might as well have asked me that question in Mandarin, for all the sense it makes to me. He smiles, says that *Inception* got him thinking of it.

"How?" I ask him. "That movie's about dreams, not parallel realities."

"Well, yeah, but it's about the subconscious and I've always been kind of fascinated by that. I mean, how often do you dream about the people you know in your actual day-to-day life? You'd think they'd be the 'stars' of the movies in your head at night, but usually, they're not. Most of the time, you're hanging out with a bunch of strangers you've never seen before, who look nothing like anybody you've ever met in your life — but they always somehow feel super familiar. You never need a" — his voice drops very low — "'previously, on *Charlotte's Subconsciousness*' recap to tell you who's who and what's going on. In the dream, you always know, don't you?"

"I suppose," I say, with a shrug. Mistake growls at the movement, clumsily turning in my arms as if to remind me who's really the boss here. "So, what are you saying? That, in dreams, we travel to other dimensions?"

He shrugs back, his cheeks flushing a little — as if, all of a sudden, he feels like an idiot for bringing up something so ... out there. I do my best to keep my expression open, encouraging, let him know that he can say anything — but I worry that the slight smile I put on comes off like I'm mocking him.

"There has to be *some* reason," he says, "why it all feels so familiar when you're in it. I dunno — maybe I'm just talking out of my ass."

His jaw clenches as he looks away. I hate myself for noting a difference between him and Colin — Anthony seems to care what I think of him, and I like that. I nudge his elbow with mine, prompt him: "Go on …"

He closes his eyes, lightly shakes his head as if saying to himself, *I can't believe I'm actually going to talk about this.* "It's not *traveling*, obviously — you never *go* anywhere. But I always wake up and wonder — what if, in the dream, I'm seeing through the eyes of some Alternate Me? Living *his* life, for a little while? Because there has to be a *reason* you never dream that you're someone else, right? You're always you, it's just the circumstances around you that are different. There's no restriction on what you can dream about, but the one thing your mind never does is give you a completely new identity. Why *wouldn't* your subconsciousness make you over into a completely new, better person?"

I'm aware that I'm staring at him now, and I just hope that my face doesn't show the question I'm afraid to ask him: *Is that what he wants? To be someone different?*

Instead, I say: "Huh … Well, okay, let's assume that is what we do when we dream, so this would obviously mean the Other Us … must be dreaming about us when they go to sleep, right?"

He laughs, looks at his shoes. I worry that, pretty soon, his cheeks are going to look almost sunburnt. "Forget it. I'm talking bollocks … Did I use that right?"

I'm not going to let him change the subject. "You just got me thinking … One of the things that always bothers me — and this happens every bloody day — is, like, when I go downstairs to the kitchen to get something, by the time I get down there, I can't remember what it is I wanted."

He nods at me. "And you feel like —"

"Like I'm waking up or something. Now you've got me wondering, what if that's what it is? Other Me, somewhere out there" — I point at what is supposed to be Another Dimension but is really just the Williamsburg Wanker in the black cardi sitting opposite, trying not to look like he's totally eavesdropping — "woke up, and it's that severed connection that has made me all confused? I think that's a far better explanation than that I'm losing my marbles at the age of seventeen."

He just smiles at me, the flush fading from his cheeks. I keep my eyes on his, trying to keep him engaged in the conversation, because his attention is on someone who is not Maya. This is the point of this whole escapade, after all.

The next thing we know, we're at 116th Street, Columbia University. We get off the train and exit the station and walk to the Upper West Side address that Katie gave me, where this party is supposed to be happening. I stay close to Anthony and let him guide me, so that I don't have to do much looking up …

So that I don't do any staring at the campus, thinking about what could be …

What might not be.

*

It takes a few presses of the buzzer and me sending Katie an SOS via WhatsApp, but we're eventually buzzed in, and I lead Anthony into the elevator and up to the fourth floor — the American *fifth* floor — of a swanky apartment building. I guess I'm in the lead because I'm the one who knows somebody at this party. The elevator lets us out. The door to 5B is open, the chatter of the guests riding a wave of indie music — because, of course — and Mistake paws at my arms as if trying to run away. I soothe her, promising we won't stay here long, as we walk into a living, breathing poster for the nonexistent J.Crew/Hollister merger.

Nothing but crisp Oxford shirts, Fair Isle sweaters and swing dresses
— preppy central! Also, they've all clustered by the front door, which
— with my tote bag and Anthony's backpack — makes getting into the
apartment a bit of a challenge.

"Oh, my badness!" Katie's voice slices through the music and the
hubbub, a deep kind of rasp that is unerringly commanding. The crowd
by the front door seems to part at its sound, giving me a view of Katie,
standing in the kitchen at the end of the hallway — counters and cup-
boards orbiting a black granite breakfast bar. She's staring at Mistake,
and I briefly panic and wonder if it's a violation of some social code to
bring an English bulldog to a Cool Party, but then Katie steps out of the
kitchen, hands extended as if to take Mistake, and I am about to hand
her the puppy when Katie actually takes hold of *me*.

"Let me see you in the light," she gasps, pulling me into the kitchen.
She holds me at arm's length, looking me up and down. "I like this
new you, Lottie." (She has called me Lottie since my first day at Sacred
Heart. I started hating it on the second day.)

"Just trying something different, you know?" I tell her, cuddling
Mistake — Katie's voice seems to be unnerving the dog. Maybe, if I
keep talking, she will calm down. "Thanks for inviting me. A party
on Christmas Eve — we don't do that back home. Is it an American
thing?"

Katie shrugs. "Nah, not really — my family's Jewish, so we don't
make a big deal out of Christmas at all. This is my cousin's apartment,
and she's out of town."

"Don't tell me she doesn't know this is happening?"

Katie's laugh is an *actual* titter. "No, no, silly — I'm bad, but I'm not
that bad. Naomi's always been cool about us having parties when she's
away. She says they're a way to experience life in fast-forward."

"What does that mean?"

She makes a face — wrinkling her nose, lightly shaking her head.

"I actually have no idea. But whatever — free party venue. Speaking of which, want to try this spiked cider that my girl Harriet cooked up?"

Katie doesn't even wait for my answer. She's already picking up a red cup from the breakfast bar, which she then hands to me. I take it, turning to ask Anthony if he'd like one, too …

But Anthony's not next to me anymore. My surprise must show on my face, because Katie points to the living room. "I think I saw him get picked off."

I wriggle my way past the gay couple canoodling under the mistletoe over the kitchen door, avoid eye contact with a jock type who I think I recognize from Biology … I'm tempted to hold up Mistake as a shield, in case he has any ideas about a "lean in." Then I think myself a monster for considering using the pup like that.

I get into the living room and almost heave at the damp air, thick with body heat, layered with the tang of spilled alcohol. I look for Anthony in the crowd and find him in a corner, by the obscenely large TV, which is on, muted, showing a rerun of *The Big Bang Theory*.

Katie was right — he's been picked off. Two girls in super cute flannel shirts and jeans — I warm to them for breaking the swing dress mold — stand in front of him. They have their backs to me, so I can't tell if they're from Sacred Heart — but what I *do* know is that they've coordinated their flirting. The one on my left, Anthony's right, works her braids through her fingertips, like she's playing a flute. The other — Anthony's left, my right — has her hands on her hips, staring at Anthony intently, not moving *at all*. She's like a mannequin, just with a healthy glow to her complexion.

"No *way* are you from Bensonhurst!" says The Mannequin, flicking a slap at Anthony's upper arm, as if telling him off for lying.

Anthony grins and looks down at his shoes. I can't tell if this is embarrassment or if he's really enjoying himself — just like I can't tell if this twinge I've got in my chest is actual jealousy.

Then I remind myself, *This is good. He needs to get over Maya.* But The Mannequin kind of looks like Maya the Sequel, and I think about rescuing him.

"I am, I swear," he says to them. "I'll prove it to you. Check this out." Then he makes sounds that I think might be words, but it's hard to tell. All I catch is "Yo."

The two girls think it's hysterical, though. Maya the Sequel says that she loves accents — Anthony's is "really, like, *real*, you know?"

"Yeah, but still," says the Hair Fiddler, "I've never met any guy from Bensonhurst who dresses like this."

"I like it." Maya the Sequel slaps his arm again — such a nuanced, versatile gesture. "Brooklyn boy gone slightly preppy. Tough and preppy." Then she gasps, stops swaying. "*Treppy!*"

The Hair Fiddler gasps. "Love. It!"

"Right?!"

Anthony smiles at them. "No, you're right — that's not my accent, not really. I am from Bensonhurst, though, I promise." Then he notices me. "Hey, you ladies want to hear a *real* accent? Check this out. Charlotte ..." He beckons me over, and there's something about the expressions on the girls' faces that makes me not want to go over. But I do.

"This is Bianca" — he points to the Hair Fiddler, then to Maya the Sequel — "and Ashley."

The two girls totally size me up for the one-and-a-half seconds they stop gazing at Anthony to look at me. They must conclude I'm not competition. As annoying as I find this, I'm also disappointed.

"Say things." Anthony's looking at me, but with the same expression I give my dog, Rocky, when I want him to show people he can nod his head "yes" and shake his head "no."

"What sort of things?" I ask.

The only answer I get is three Americans badly echoing me: "'Wot sawt uh fings?'"

All three of them laugh at their bad impressions, and I start to hope I get deported. If this is what I have to look forward to from next year on ...

Anthony stops laughing long enough to reach for Mistake. "Want me to take her off your hands so you can enjoy that drink?"

As soon as Mistake is in Anthony's arms, Bianca and Ashley start cooing — not over the amazingly cute dog, but at how "adorable" Anthony looks cuddling her. They didn't react to the dog *at all* when she was in my arms.

I also can't help noticing that Anthony has been smiling the whole time I've been in the living room, which must be entirely due to Bianca and Ashley. For a second, I feel an urge to snatch Mistake back. Is that all it takes? A couple of hot girls flash their teeth, bat their eyes, and he's no longer heartbroken? Was he ever heartbroken? Or was I the only one feeling something real?

But ... this *was* the point. Getting him over Maya.

It seems to be working.

Bianca's pointing from Anthony to me and back again. "So, what is this? This your girlfriend?"

"No!" says Anthony — a little quick. A little *loud*.

"I'm going to go talk to some of the girls from Sacred Heart," I tell him. "You okay with Mistake?"

I don't wait for his answer. I turn around and start toward the living room door. Then I stop dead, my legs feeling like they've been turned to concrete, my heart doing its level best to climb right out of my chest, beating out a dubstep rhythm the whole time. I genuinely feel like I might pass out as I stare at a slightly lanky, very pale boy in a black cardigan over a white T-shirt for some band called The National, standing in the doorway between the living room and the kitchen.

My ex-boyfriend, Colin. He's *here*.

So much for Step Six!

"You okay, Charlotte?" Anthony tears his attention away from Bianca and Ashley to see why I'm being so weird all of a sudden.

I turn to look at him, hoping my fake grin covers up the grimace I can feel tugging at my cheeks, but pretty sure I'm just managing a *grinace*. "Yep, fine, just trying to figure out how I can get past all those people by the door. There's a lot of them. It'll be a squeeze. I might spill my cider." And now I'm rambling!

He's looking at me funny, but Bianca and Ashley have converged on Mistake, and I don't want to distract him from his distraction. He's moving on, his ex being forced right out of his head — which is great for him.

Bless his heart, Anthony ignores the two hot girls and focuses only on me, giving me a look that asks if I'm sure I'm okay. I do my best *Oh-I'm-fine* face when, really, I know that if my expression had subtitles, they'd say: "Uh, no, I'm not okay. Colin, the arsehole I came here to avoid talking about, is *here* at this party. Yes, of course he's the one in the skinny jeans — how did you know? I'm totally, totally freaking out, and I kind of want to leave this party right now, but I can also see that you're having fun, and I don't know why, but I don't like that. This is one giant emotional overload, and I don't know if it'll be my heart or my head that explodes first!"

God, I even ramble in my mind.

But I don't say any of this to him. Instead, I just keep grinacing and give him a nod, then turn back to the door. Colin's moved on. I make my way to the kitchen — mercifully, Colin's not there (he must have joined the front-door crowd). I leave my cider untouched on the breakfast bar, then lean on the worktop at the far wall, trying to get myself together. It's only now that I'm having this emotional overload that I realize I've been doing pretty well these last few hours. Distraction was kind of working — but it won't work now that I'm sharing physical space with him.

What is he even doing here? This party is far too mainstream for him. I think the song I can hear coming from the living room is a James Bay song, which should be causing Colin to break out in hives or something. Also, I don't remember him talking to Katie at school, ever, so why would he even be invited?

But then, pretty much the only thing I *do* remember right now is the last time I saw him. It was a week ago, at school, on the last day of the semester — one week after he'd dumped me.

I was standing at my locker, feeling frustrated that I'd forgotten what I was there for — maybe an Alternate Me woke up from what I imagine was a very boring dream — and extremely annoyed at the clanging and banging of all the lockers slamming shut up and down the hallway. I'd had classes all that morning, but whatever I'd learned in them had fallen right out of my head, because the only thing I was able to focus on was the memory of Colin telling me that he needed to feel *passion* for the girl he was with. Each time I'd reached the end of the mental replay, I'd rewind to the beginning, and the more and more I did that, the worse and worse his breakup line would get. I couldn't stop myself from rewriting the scene so that he'd actually *explain* what he meant:

"I just need to feel excitement — like, all the time. Constantly. Every day. And I just never feel that with you, Charlotte. I've tried — believe me, I have *so* tried — but it's just not there. You're like a small candle, but I want a real *fire*. You know?"

It was while I was halfway through a third rerun of this moment — when I was remembering-but-really-imagining (*remegining*) him comparing me to a gentle drought when he wanted a tornado — that I noticed, oh God, he was walking over to me.

Breezy casual, Charlotte, I told myself. *Breezy casual.*

He stopped right in front of me, stuffing his hands into his jeans pockets, hunching his shoulders and looking at the lockers. "Hey,

Charm," he said. I wished that he wouldn't use the nickname he'd settled on only a week before he'd dumped me. At the same time, I felt a happy swell in my chest — if he was still using it, then maybe …

"You going home tomorrow?" he asked the locker.

"No … No …" There was so much more to my answer, but everything I wanted to say rushed to the front of my brain, all at the same time. Thoughts and feelings tripped over each other, just before they reached my mouth, leaving me standing there dumbly — going for breezy casual and missing by miles. If there was one thing that conversation definitely was not, it was breezy casual.

Well, actually, that's not true — *Colin* was certainly breezy and casual. He kept on looking at the locker as he said there was something he had to ask me.

He's going to take me back, I thought. *That's why he asked when I was leaving — he's realizing what it means. He's freaking out about never seeing me again. Okay, you can get through this, Charm — just don't seem too relieved when he asks you. You've got to ride out the pause a little bit, let him sweat — let him realize, you don't need to get back with him. You don't need —*

"Did you finish *Infinite Jest*? Can I have it back?"

I stared at him, my mouth going dry. I wondered, would it be possible to stuff myself in one of the lockers? We don't have lockers in schools back home, but American TV shows always had bullied kids being stuffed into lockers. They must have been super skinny boys, though, because I'd have to dislocate a few joints if I was going to have any chance of fitting.

As Colin looked at me then, my anger and hurt melded together, creating a kind of hot nausea in my belly. I couldn't decide whether to cry, scream at or throw up on him. A week had gone by since he'd broken my heart, and the only thing he wanted to talk about was a book he wanted back — a book he'd claimed to love but I could tell he'd never finished.

"Yeah," I said. It had been my turn to look at the locker. "I'll get it to you."

"You don't have to bring it to my house or anything," he said. A little quick. "I don't think that'd be a good idea for either of us. Especially you."

"Huh?"

"Well, yeah, 'cause … You seem kind of emotional still. Just … I don't know, give it to one of the girls. They can give it to me after the holidays. I'll see you around, okay?"

Yeah, he actually said he'd see me "around," like we had a chance of bumping into each other on the street anytime soon. But what hurt worse was what he did next. Started to walk away, then stopped just long enough to say: "I had fun."

Then he took another step, stopped and turned back again: "It was fun."

One more step, one more stop. "*You* were fun."

Okay, there was only one step, only one stop. He said he'd had fun, and then he walked away. But right now, standing in the kitchen of Katie's cousin's apartment, a party going on around me, I'm remegining the last time I saw my ex-boyfriend, making his parting shot crueler, his face colder, because …

Because what? Because I'm afraid that was all I was to him. Fun. I thought he loved me. I *know* I loved him. I feel a sharp, hot fury in my chest, like I've swallowed a mouthful of thorns, as I wonder — why did it take me two weeks to accept that "fun" was *such* a shitty thing for him to say?

I hear the clatter of heels on linoleum. Katie stumbles into the kitchen, stopping to lean against the fridge. She's almost pulling off the *I'm-so-not-really-drunk* look. She sees me, pulls a frown: "Didn't you have a dog?"

"My friend's holding her." I think about just gulping down the cider, but what would be the point? The alcohol can't wash away the thorns in my chest, can't erase the memory of Colin and what he said to me.

"What's up?" Katie starts to step away from the fridge, then reconsiders. "You look kind of stressed."

"It's nothing," I say. "I just …" *If I say it, I'm talking about him, and I will fail Step Six.* But I need to tell someone. "I got weirded out when I saw … Colin." Fail.

Now Katie steps away from the fridge, her eyes alert and sober. "He's here? Where?"

"I don't know — the hall, I guess. You know, you could have warned me you'd invited him." And what's with the *look*? Is she … excited that Colin's here?

"Oh, come on, sweetie. I know it might be kind of awkward to run into someone you fooled around with, but it doesn't *have* to be."

I know that I've started to freak out when I register that the mute button in my head has turned on, the music that I had been hearing behind me dropping to nothing. For a moment, the only sound I hear is Katie's voice, three words echoing in my brain.

… fooled around with …

I THOUGHT HE LOVED ME, I scream inside my brain. But before the words can force themselves out of my lips, I catch the end of Katie's sentence.

"— besides, you brought a date to this party, so you're clearly over it."

The only noise I make is an indignant gasp, and before I can form words, Colin seems to materialize, passing by me without even noticing, taking Katie by the hand and pulling her in for a kiss — deep, firm, *passionate.*

Oh my God. Any drowsy feeling the cider gave me evaporates in seconds, and I feel like I've been plunged into ice water.

I make a second indignant gasp, and Colin pauses mid-kiss, his lips still on hers as he turns his head. He looks right at me and breaks away from Katie like her tongue just gave him an electric shock.

He stares at the ground for a second, nods to himself and looks back up. He taps the tip of Katie's nose with his finger, affectionate and possessive. "I need to talk to Charlotte," he tells her, beckoning me to follow him to the back of the kitchen and out onto the balcony.

I don't *want* to follow him out. He's not going to take me back. Even if I hadn't seen him and Katie together, he made that pretty clear at the lockers last week. But even so, I find myself kind of *needing* to know what it is he has to say.

And when I see that Katie tries — but fails — to keep the giddy smile off her face, I think that even out there in the cold, with him, is better than being in this bloody kitchen.

So, I follow him out onto the balcony. It's a small space, and the up-turned deck table forces us to stand close together, side by side, craning our necks to see each other as we look out over Broadway. Traffic is lazily flowing, snow is lazily falling. It's kind of beautiful — but also bloody cold. I tighten my scarf, zip up the leather jacket.

"I like this," he says, gesturing at my new ensemble. I feel a warmth in my chest and wish that I didn't. He doesn't get to make me feel good anymore. "But, seriously, what are you still doing here? I thought you were going home yesterday."

"It was today, actually," I tell him. God, he really didn't know when I was going home. Did he ever listen to me at all? "But my flight got canceled, and so I'm stranded here."

He makes a pained face, like he really, really pities me. I'm surprised he doesn't reach out and stroke my hair comfortingly. I'm annoyed to realize I'd kind of like it if he did. "You're stranded in New York, yeah — but you're not stranded at a party you knew I'd be at. You *chose* to come here."

It's the third time I've made the same indignant gasp. It's starting to irritate me — I don't want to go back to being English Charlotte full time until I'm actually back in England. "I did *not* know you'd be here. If I did, believe me, I wouldn't have come anywhere near —"

"This is not *healthy*, Charlotte. It's hard to have an attachment to something an ocean away. You need to start getting over it. I mean, come on, it's been two weeks — how much longer do you need?"

How much longer do I need? Does he seriously think that two weeks is long enough to get over not only the relationship but also the loss of the future that I was imagining? Where is the boy who cut the line in the cafeteria so that we could sit together? Who said very little when we had lunch, because he "just wanted to listen" to my voice? Who bought me simple but classy notepads to write in?

The boy who chased me at the start of the semester has been body snatched by an arrogant, aloof git — the eager, interested expression he used to have when he looked at me has been replaced by a cringe, signaling that this is all just a big inconvenience ... to *him*.

But why do I still want him to reach out and touch me?

I know I should end this conversation right now. It's not going anywhere good and may actually result in my Story becoming some kind of pathetic comedy that ends with me being put on trial for assaulting this git, the judge laughing as he hears how I knocked him over the balcony with my tote bag of all things. For one thing, I'm not sure I'll be allowed a laptop in jail.

Colin starts talking again. "I tried for a month to get you to see that it wasn't serious. Well, not to me. We were fooling around for a couple of months while you were here. You were always going to go home, so it wasn't any kind of forever thing, you know?"

"I must have been sleeptalking when we 'decided' that."

He's starting to get agitated. I know this because he's actually taken off his beanie. "I thought you understood. I thought you were, like, cool."

"And *I* thought we loved each other."

He gives me a look like I've suddenly started speaking Elvish, and

I think I must be the biggest idiot in the history of idiots for coming out here when I should have stayed in the kitchen — or gone back to the living room and demanded that Anthony stop talking to the two flirters and get me out of this apartment. But it's out there now. I've humbled myself and might as well finish this conversational seppuku:

"Well, that's what you *said*, anyway. Whether you meant it or not —"

"I *never* told you I loved you." His insistence is as firm as when Anthony made it clear to Bianca and Ashley that we were not together. What is it — am I unthinkable? Is that the case with everyone, or just New York boys?

"You did." I force myself to hold eye contact with him. "The fountain, Lincoln Center —"

"No. You told *me* that you loved me, but I *never* said it back."

Okay, he's just rewriting history now. But *I* remember it clearly. Our first time in the city together: We'd been dating — *not* "fooling around" — for about a month, and I asked him to take me to Lincoln Center. I hoped that he wouldn't figure out I kind of wanted to go there only because of *Pitch Perfect*. I remember thinking that I had made a fool of myself by getting excited when I saw the fountain for the first time, practically dragging Colin forward a few steps as I rushed it like a little kid, weaving in and out of tourists, ruining at least three photographs.

He was laughing that day, as we got to the fountain. I remember that very clearly, just like I remember the soft spray from the arcing water. The amazement that someone could make room in Manhattan — cramped, clustered, cluttered Manhattan — for this beautiful mess of stone and glass that surrounded the fountain and courtyard on three sides. How, if you turned away from Columbus Avenue, somehow the noise of the traffic just went away ...

I was so in love with New York at that moment and so in love with

Colin that the words were out of my mouth before I'd even managed to successfully interlace his fingers with mine.

"I love this," I said. "And I love you."

And he said …

"Yeah …"

Yeah.

Oh, bollocks. I *don't* remember him saying it back to me. I must have just remegined it, because how could it be possible for me to fall in love with someone who wasn't in love with me as well? Isn't that what falling — *being* — "in love" is? "In love" = two people who love *each other*, doesn't it?

"I think you should go." His face — all sharp lines and haunted hazel eyes — is stern now. He's not telling me to leave for my own good, he's telling me to leave because, as he says, "It's the worst idea in the world for us to be around each other right now. And since this is Katie's party — she invited me weeks ago — it's not fair to her if *I* go. I really don't want to disappoint her."

The thorns in my chest start wriggling, and I feel like I could projectile vomit all over him. Okay, he didn't love me back, but does he have to be so blatant about his priorities now? Is he *trying* to hurt me? *I do not deserve this!*

"We got a problem?"

Anthony's here — and he's letting a little bit of the Brooklyn voice he put on for Bianca and Ashley creep into his own. He's standing in the doorway — he must be part ninja to have snuck up so quietly — with a sleeping Mistake in his arms, staring at Colin with a kind of blank expression.

Colin looks at me. "Who's this guy?"

Where would I start? Fortunately, Anthony's got this. "That's not an answer to my question. All I want to know is, are you bothering my friend?"

"Bothering your ..." Colin looks at me, like, *What is he talking about?*

I just shrug at him, the prickly feeling in my chest starting to fade a little. I'm curious to see what happens here.

Colin scoffs, putting his beanie back on — the hipster equivalent of a power move. "I'm not bothering anybody, okay? If anything, she's bothering me. But it's all okay, because Charlotte was just leaving."

"I don't think she was," says Anthony. "Besides, I'm having a good time and, more importantly, so's my dog."

All three of us look at Mistake, whose nose twitches as she snores loudly. I almost laugh in spite of my discomfort, my heavy heart.

Now, Colin looks at Anthony. "'Ev." Ugh, I forgot about his butchering of "Whatever." There goes my smile. "Anyway, screw that — me and Charlotte already agreed she'd leave."

We did?

Anthony shakes his head. "I highly doubt that."

Colin looks at me to intervene. "What's this guy's problem?"

I bite the inside of my cheeks to keep from smiling and showing Colin how much I'm suddenly enjoying this. "It looks like you are."

Colin actually stamps his foot. "You know what? I'm sick of this. You guys should take off before you kill this party for everybody else."

Mistake's stirring, and Anthony absently pets her head. It should look totally ridiculous, but it somehow just makes him look even more in control of this conversation.

"I don't feel like going anywhere," he says. "And where I come from, people only leave a place when someone makes them. You gonna do that?"

"This is so primitive!" Colin's voice is a squeak, and he looks like he'd make for the door if only there was a route that didn't take him through Anthony. "You really resorting to threats, dude?"

"Who made any threats?"

I take Anthony's hand, wrapping my fingers around his palm and, for a second, enjoying the idea of Colin wondering, *Hey, is she* with *this guy?* "Come on, it's time to go."

For the first time since he's been out here, Anthony stops eyeballing Colin and looks at me. Up close, I'm relieved to see that he really does seem to be in control — he's not just pretending. "Are you sure?" he asks.

I keep my voice small, because — for some reason — I want only Anthony to hear this next bit. "I *am*. I'm done here."

He squeezes my hand. We walk back into Katie's party without saying a word more to Colin, not even acknowledging Bianca and Ashley as we pass them in the kitchen. I'm feeling good, like I've cleaned out my heart, taken out garbage I should have dumped two weeks ago — garbage I shouldn't have collected in the first place.

As we walk, still hand in hand, down the four flights of stairs to street level, I'm feeling somehow cleaner on the inside. Looser, lighter …

*

About three minutes later, I'm crying on 116th Street.

"I'm sorry," I tell Anthony, as he brushes snow off a stoop and motions for me to sit down. He plonks himself beside me and squeezes my hand. He hasn't let go since the balcony.

"It's okay, really," he whispers.

Without thinking, I lean my head on his shoulder, and something about the comfort of doing this must relax me enough to start weeping into his field coat. Mistake wriggles in my arms, whining and desperately climbing up my chest, because it seems to be very important for me to get face licks.

They do actually make me feel a little bit better.

"She's worried about you." I can hear the smile in Anthony's voice.

Feel him shift slightly, his head turning toward mine, his nose brushing against my hair.

His arm against mine stiffens, as he catches himself. His head turns away from me as he whispers, "So am I."

My cheeks flush, but I think that's just from the crying. I reach up to wipe my nose with the back of my hand, then stop myself. Am I *that* comfortable with a boy I met less than six hours ago?

"What is it?" Anthony asks me.

I give him the honest answer. "I'm just realizing what a complete idiot I've been."

I run through the story: Colin and me, at the fountain at Lincoln Center, a clear night that wasn't too cold, the hand-in-hand running through tourists, me telling him how I felt … saying I loved him.

I feel Anthony's head nod against mine. "But he didn't say it back."

"I thought that he did … I thought that, because I loved him, he had to love me back. You know?" Screw it. I wipe my nose. Sniffle loudly, grossly. Cry some more. "But I guess you were right in the airport … Maybe I don't understand love … Maybe I never d-d-d —"

I shut up, because if I don't, I'll probably sob. I grit my teeth, make that wet, inward sighing sound you do when you're strangling a wail. Were it not for Anthony letting go of my hand and putting his arm around me like a brace, I think I'd actually let go, and start properly crying, with shaking shoulders and everything. I'm almost proud of myself for keeping it down to simple sniffles and single tears — a respectable form of weeping. Mistake just burrows into the crook of my arm, and I clutch at her as if drawing power.

This might be the most bizarre group hug ever seen on the Upper West Side.

Anthony — bless him — gives me a long minute to get myself together. When I've calmed down, he says:

"Listen, whatever it is, whatever you're trying to … I don't know, hold in … don't. You're seventeen. It's okay to cry when you have a reason."

I wish he didn't say that — permission drags open the floodgates a little more, and I put my face in my free hand, feeling lines of tears and snot quickly run down my wrist. Anthony holds me to him, tighter. My heart's still hurting, but a relaxed calm comes over me at the same time, enough of a calm to get me to admit something.

"I guess I shouldn't have prewritten my New York Story."

He speaks into my hair. "What do you mean?"

Sniff. Sniff. Sigh. "I mean, I came here with the Story already written in my head. I was going to have the best time, because I could be me — or a version of me I don't get to be back home. And by being that 'me,' I was going to" — I feel like I might literally choke on the next words — "attract somebody. I'd been failing at that all through school, but I'd convinced myself I wasn't the problem, the problem was that I belonged somewhere else. I just needed to be in a place where I did belong, and then someone would *get* me. Now, I feel like an idiot, because if I hadn't got so wrapped up in what I imagined *would* happen, maybe I'd have paid more attention to what was *happening*. But that's me, I guess … Never in the moment, never impulsive."

"And that's why you want to be impulsive today?"

I laugh, hoping he doesn't notice the flecks of spittle splattering his field coat. "Pretty lame, huh? I can be impulsive when there's next to no consequences."

His fingers quickly squeeze my shoulder twice — an encouraging, comforting gesture. "Don't sell yourself short. That impulsive decision not to go to the hotel got you stranded in Manhattan in the middle of the night, and you're currently risking hypothermia sitting still for so long. I'd say that's a consequence."

"Yeah, I suppose …"

We lapse into silence for a few seconds, until Anthony asks me: "You really feel like you don't belong back home?"

"I don't know," I admit. "I'm starting to think, maybe it's not so much that I feel like I don't belong back home, more that I ..." I shrug, to show I at least know that what I'm about to say might be lame — and even kind of childishly selfish. "I guess part of me wants more."

"That's not something to feel bad about."

I lean away so that I can look at him. He keeps his hand on me. "So, what now?" I ask. "Take the next step?"

"You know, I was thinking maybe we take a time-out from the book. In fact ..." He pulls away but keeps his arm around me. He looks me up and down. "I don't think we need a time-out. I think we need a reset. I mean, you look amazing in this outfit, but ..."

He looks away, and his teeth clamp on his bottom lip. Seeing him shy, after he's just intimidated my ex-boyfriend into becoming a jittery, squeaky fool, is a bit disconcerting.

I lean forward, cursing myself for sniffling still. "What?"

His lips curl in a rueful smile. He shakes his head, as if not believing what he's about to say. "I was just going to tell you that, actually, I think I liked your original look better. Now that I've gotten to know you a little bit, it feels more ... you, I guess."

I look down at myself and nod. "Yeah, I guess I haven't done this tough girl look any sort of justice. Okay ... Let's reboot, then."

I look up and down 116th Street. "It's after nine on Christmas Eve. Everything's closed, right? Where can we go to change?"

"I guess we could go to a bar. They're pretty much the only places open."

I tut. "I'm underage, even back home. And so are you."

He takes his arm away from me to reach into his inside pocket. Takes out a driver's license and shows it to me. It's a recent picture of him, but the license *says* it's about two years old, and that Anthony is twenty-three, nearly twenty-four.

I'm impressed. "That looks a *lot* more convincing than some of the ones I've seen at Sacred Heart."

"I know a guy" is the only explanation he gives me.

"Well, that's great for you, but I only have my passport, and that has my *real* date of birth on it."

"The place I'm thinking of doesn't card hot girls." He puts the ID back in his pocket, keeps his arm to himself. I'm more aware of its absence than I should be.

"We can go to a bar," I say, "but I'm not sure alcohol is the best idea for me right now. Not after …" I trail off because, damn it, I don't have to fail Step Six any harder than I already have.

"Sure." He gets up, dusts some snow off his shoulders. "All I want is to be somewhere warm. We can have one drink, get ourselves together and then keep stepping." He holds out his hand.

I shift Mistake from one side to the other so that I don't reach for him with the hand I used to wipe my nose. "Where are we going?"

"To my favorite dive bar."

6. ~~GO TWENTY-FOUR HOURS WITHOUT MENTIONING YOUR EX.~~

(Kind of.)

~ CHAPTER SIX ~

ANTHONY

9:35 P.M.

Most of Hell's Kitchen has gentrified enough to need rebranding, but the streets behind Port Authority are still worthy of the name. Because of this, I stand protectively close to Charlotte as we walk along Fortieth Street, willing my arm not to slink around her shoulders, holding her to me. *She's not Maya, she's not my girlfriend, she's not anything …*

Well, that's not actually true. She's not nothing. I don't know what she *is*, but she's not nothing. And it's nice to feel this again — the closeness of someone who *wants* to be close to you. I don't remember the last time I felt that way with Maya.

"I know you said this place was a dive," Charlotte says, as the neon-blue sign for the bar looms into view. "But should I do something about our dog?"

"Yeah, probably a good idea to keep her hidden," I answer, and as Charlotte wrestles and wriggles Mistake into her tote bag, I realize she said "*our*" dog, and I can tell from the way she doesn't look at me after she's gotten Mistake hidden away that she's realized it, too. But it's only weird if we actually talk about it, so I don't talk about it.

As I predicted, my fake ID and Charlotte's looks get us right past the bouncer — who is far more interested in the epic text message he's writing, anyway. Charlotte opens the door, and we head inside. I can't help stealing a look at what the bouncer's writing. I catch at least two "Sorrys" and one "I messed up, and I gotta live with that."

At least *some* people who cheat actually feel bad about it.

Not only is Ice Bar a dive, it's also about as dead as Elvis tonight. There's a lanky guy — who I guess is in his midthirties — sitting in the classic elbows-on-the-bar, head-over-whiskey pose that I'm surprised to see in real life. At a booth in the back, a forty-something woman (who might be a Goth, but it might also be the light in here) is staring at two wineglasses in front of her. Hers is half full, the other is empty, as if whoever she was with earlier drained it and made a quick exit. Brutal.

At another booth, a jock-type guy is flicking through the photos on his phone, lingering on each for a second, then moving to the next. Behind him, a twenty-something couple — one of those annoyingly perfect ones, each so good-looking they actually start to look like siblings — are sitting across from each other, limply holding hands and staring at the table. A breakup's happening. Bing Crosby is finishing up about being home for Christmas, but that seems to be a problem for everyone in here. Charlotte can't go home, and everyone else — including me — is probably dreading it.

"I'm not sure this is going to do much for our moods," Charlotte mumbles.

I shrug. "Well, at least we can take comfort in the fact that we're doing better than most of the people in here."

She shrugs back and mumbles, "I guess."

I let her know that we can duck into the bathroom and change — and if it's still dead when we're done, we can take off.

She agrees, as Bing makes way for George Michael's "Last Christmas," and I realize that this might totally be my song *next* Christmas. The difference is that Maya didn't so much give my heart away — the very next day — as see how far she could throw it. Emotionally, that girl's got some arm on her.

I catch Charlotte's eye and can tell from the slight smirk on her face — half pain, half humor — that she's thinking the same thing as me. *Of all the songs to be playing as we walk in …*

I look to her. "Meet you back out here?"

Charlotte nods, and we both head to the bathrooms, which are scarily pristine for a bar that otherwise looks like it's survived a nuclear war. The first time I saw the bathroom here was at the start of the semester when my college buddy Tom and I were test-driving our fake IDs. I'd had a few beers by the time I headed to the bathroom, and I freaked out, thinking that I'd either gone into the ladies' room (as they're supposedly much nicer, as a rule) or a whole new bar. Tom got worried because I didn't come out again for five whole minutes.

I change quickly, mindful to keep the bought clothes carefully folded, although I'm maybe not as confident in our chances of returning them as I told Charlotte. Well, *my* chances of returning them, I remind myself, because I'm the one who's still going to be here to make the trip back to Macy's. She's going home — for Christmas — tomorrow.

Once I'm changed, I tuck the folded Macy's gear back into my backpack and eye myself in the mirror, wondering, *what the hell am I thinking, bringing a nice girl to Ice Bar?*

But my stomach isn't churning from worry that I'll get back out there and Charlotte will have taken off. This is weird — I mean, do I not care what she thinks? I took Maya to far classier places than this and spent half the time thinking I was going to be dumped at any moment — particularly if a place was as dead as Ice Bar is tonight. Maya could never appreciate a quiet establishment. There always needed to be other people … because then there'd be a better chance of finding a replacement for me? (*Damn, Anthony, let it go.*) But I'm not panicking about what Charlotte thinks of this dead dive bar in Hell's Kitchen.

I guess I'm just that comfortable around her.

Charlotte's already at the bar when I go back in, once again wearing the clothes she had on when we met. They are definitely more her, but how did I lose a quick-change race to a girl? How *long* did I stare at myself in the mirror? She's taken a seat three stools down from the guy hunched over his whiskey, with Mistake dozing on the floor next to her, in her tote bag. I instinctively put my body between her and him, although I don't know what, exactly, I'm shielding her from.

"Want a Coke or something?" I ask her.

She shakes her head, but she's smiling, and I'm so psyched to see it — after she was sniveling less than twenty minutes ago — that I'm ready to buy her whatever she wants. Except I have no idea what she means when she says she wants "a drink with a little brolly in it."

She cracks up at my clueless look and explains that a brolly is not another cute British curse. "Y'know, a parasol. An *umbrella.*"

"I know what a parasol is," I tell her, motioning to the bartender. "It was 'brolly' that confused me." I order a beer for myself and a virgin mojito for Charlotte. It doesn't come with a little parasol, and when the bartender moves off, she makes a face at me.

"Not that kind of place," I say.

She taps her fingers on the bar, thinking. Then she reaches for a coaster, checking that it's dry. She folds it a couple times, then balances it on top of her straw. She leans back in her stool.

"There." She grins at me. "Since we've already improvised so much today."

The makeshift umbrella falls off, and we laugh, and I'm about to make a joke about neither of us being able to do anything right today. But I stop myself from doing that.

The playlist has shuffled to "Have Yourself a Merry Little Christmas."

"What?" Charlotte's looking at me as the song fades out. She clearly caught the look of disdain I always get whenever I hear a cover of the song.

"They wimped out," I tell her. "The last lines are supposed to be different, and much more depressing. It talks about muddling through life until the fates allow us to be together." Oh, crap, I'm so close to actually starting to sing the song.

"I didn't know that," Charlotte says.

"Most people covering the song now change the last verse. I guess they think the original is too sad or whatever. But I dunno — sometimes that's what Christmas *is* about. Muddling through, doing your best to keep it together when all the fake happiness around you just reminds you that you're *not* happy."

"Is that what your family does? Muddle through?"

"Yeah, I guess." I'm aware of my fingers tightening around the beer glass — I'm thinking about what she was saying after we left the party, about her hopes for New York becoming the place where she belonged, and what she said at Washington Square, about the idea of "home," a place I still don't want to go to right now …

I seek refuge in my beer, taking a big gulp and letting the moment pass. After a pause, I'm confident enough to look back at Charlotte, but she's looking at me with what I think is pity, because I guess she's filled in enough of the blanks. Then I see her hand start to move.

She's reaching for me. For my face. Is she making a move? I don't even know what I want to do about it if she does. But I gotta figure it out, because something might be about to happen …

She flicks the tip of my nose.

"Beer foam," she says. We both laugh, though I can also feel this weird tension in my chest starting to release. Am I … disappointed?

The moment is kind of shredded by the sound of loud, wet sniffling. I look down to where Mistake is lying, thinking that the pup might be sick or something, but she's still asleep, snoring.

Charlotte leans to look past me, farther down the bar, and then makes a face.

"I guess that proves what you were saying," she whispers to me. "Christmas is a time for muddling through."

I turn and look. The guy three stools down, bent over his whiskey, is not just a morose, moody drinker — he's wiping his eyes and nose with the backs of his fingers. His shoulders are quivering like he's being electrocuted gently.

Charlotte and I share a grimace. I have a feeling we both might know something about what he's going through, too. Then I ask Charlotte what she wants to do now. After we're done here, does she want to go back to the airport?

She frowns at me over her mocktail. "What about the steps? We've only done ..." She looks to the ceiling, mentally ticking them off. I try not to stare at those dimples and wonder why they draw my eye the way they do. "Five. That's just half."

"Well, I thought that you might be done with the book. That last step kind of blew up in our faces."

She almost sprays mojito all over me. "You *think*?" She sets her drink down, looks for a napkin. Doesn't see one. She shrugs and wipes her mouth with the back of her hand. Something Maya would never do — at least, not in front of me. "I was kind of enjoying it up until the party, though. And besides, I've still got plenty of hours to kill before my flight. I'd rather spend them seeing as much of the city as I can, rather than brooding in the airport, thinking about a certain pranny."

I laugh. "Please keep bringing the British curses! They don't make any sense at all, but I'm loving them."

She leans forward, smiling. "Pranny, bollocks, bugger, wanker, tosser, pillock, poxy."

"Okay, now you're just making sounds."

"I'm actually not. But, whatever, sod swearing — let's keep going. What?"

She's asking me why I'm grinning at her the way I am right now, but I just shake my head, choosing not to tell her that I'm impressed at how she, a girl who got knocked down so mercilessly a couple weeks ago — and then totally stomped on within the last hour — is picking herself back up. She's a fighter. I like that.

We both jump at the sound of a fist slamming on the bar, glasses rattling. The bartender — a tall, broad-shouldered gym rat who, I can tell, totally digs the standard plain black bartender's tee, because it gives everyone a ballpark figure of how much he can bench — walks over to the Crying Man. His whiskey has to be thirty percent mucus by now.

"Come on, Doug," says the bartender. "I know you're hurting, but you're bothering the other customers."

I look at Charlotte, ready to suggest we take off, but she's got *Ten Easy Steps* on her lap, and she's flicking through it.

"Seriously?"

"Just a sec," she says, still flicking. Then: "Ah! I knew I remembered seeing it — reminded me of what my mum said to me earlier ..." She turns the book over so I can see the step that we skipped: "Do something for someone worse off than you."

I look from Charlotte to Devastated Doug, who is staring into his whiskey glass as if he's hoping to find something he might have dropped in there. "I don't know," I mumble. "He might be too drunk to listen to anybody."

"Can't hurt to try," she mumbles back, returning the book to her tote bag.

Now she's nudging me down the bar, toward the Crying Man — why am *I* going first? — and when I'm up close and see his face screwed up into a ball, teeth clenched as he takes quick, wet, rasping breaths, I know that the question I'm about to ask is pointless. Of course the answer will be "No" — but there's no other way to open this conversation.

"You okay?"

Doug takes a big sniff and looks at me. Wipes his nose with his hand again. "Yeah, yeah." He sits back on his stool, picking up the glass and toying with the whiskey. "Just trying and failing to drown my sorrows." He knocks the drink back and puts the glass down gently — obviously so that the bartender will be more amenable to his thumbs-up signal for one more.

"The Doug is just in mourning," he goes on. I avoid looking at Charlotte, in case she's on the verge of laughing, too. It takes a certain something to pull off talking about yourself in the third person.

The bartender pours Doug another whiskey. "You've been trying to drown your sorrows for a week now, Doug."

"Seven years, Craig," says Doug, picking up the refilled glass then putting it right back down again. "Seven years The Doug gave that woman. That's twenty percent of his life. Twenty percent of his time on this earth was spent devoted to *her*, and she leaves him so she can go 'find herself'? What kind of crap is that?"

I shoot Charlotte a *see-what-you've-gotten-us-into* look, but she's not looking at me. She's taking the stool on the other side of Doug, who continues his rant:

"Lemme tell you, that ditz will find herself but forget to exchange email addresses. Know what I'm saying?" He sighs. "The Doug doesn't mean that. He's just letting off steam."

"Hey," says Charlotte, putting a hand on his shoulder, "you're going to get over this."

That's basically just *It'll be okay* with what feels like more substance, but I guess it's not bad. Doug isn't having it, though. He looks from Charlotte to me. "What do you two know? You look so perfect as a couple, I'll bet you've never had a fight."

"Actually, we're —"

I talk over Charlotte. I don't know why. "Oh, we fight, Doug. Believe that. But you know something? When we met, we'd both been through the worst breakups that we could imagine." Charlotte and I have a brief discussion with our eyes, behind Doug's back:

Her: *What are you doing?*

Me: *Just go with it.*

Her: *You want to lie to The Doug?*

Me: *Trust me, this is what The Doug needs right now.*

Her: *If you say so …*

I finish up. "I couldn't imagine moving on. I thought that was it and then — boom! A cool English girl throws a book at my foot, and here we are." I'm deliberately not looking at Charlotte. I maybe should have made up our meet-cute. "You never know what's gonna happen."

"That's right." Charlotte pats his shoulder. "You never know what's around the corner."

Doug's eyes brighten with hope — just for a second, before he shakes his head. "Around every corner, The Doug finds a dead end. So many dead ends."

Now I'm patting his shoulder. "So, look for a door. There's always a way out. There's always a new path. But you can't find it if you stand still, you know what I mean?"

I look at Charlotte over Doug's shoulders again. I expect her eyes to tell me she thinks I'm full of it, but she actually just gives me a single nod. She agrees.

For the first time tonight, I think that we both might *actually* be okay … eventually.

The Doug's twirling his glass as he ponders what I said. He sets the glass down without taking a sip. "The Doug's gotta take a whiz."

He gets up, shuffles off toward the bathroom. Charlotte's looking at me with a grimace. "I hate that word."

"This from the girl whose favorite curse is 'bollocks'?"

She grins as she slides off the stool. "I didn't say that was my favorite. My favorite is — *Mistake!*"

Just as I'm wondering how that could be a bad word in British English, Charlotte's barreling past me to where we were sitting before, crouching down to stop "our" dog from clambering out of her bag.

"Get back inside," she whispers. "We'll get in trouble." But Mistake isn't having it, and Charlotte takes a look at the empty bar and seems to conclude that it's worth letting her loose. If we get thrown out, so what? We were planning to leave soon, anyway. She picks Mistake up and carries her over to me.

"Do you think we're helping him?" Charlotte asks, as Mistake gets on with the business of making up for lost face licks. The gym rat bartender doesn't seem to mind at all. But then, he does seem more focused on his cell phone, in a way that makes me think he's FaceTiming with himself.

"I don't know," I tell her. "He's kinda lit, so I'm not sure how much of what we've said is sinking in. Maybe if we'd met him two or three whiskies ago."

"Pretty funny how you let him think we were together." She's looking at me, unblinking, and I can't tell if she's mad or offended or something else. She's definitely curious, maybe even a little confused.

"I just did it for The Doug," I say, hoping the self-consciousness I'm feeling doesn't translate to blushing. I try not to wonder if the tone of her voice means she thinks me unthinkable. Like, if what I told Doug was not only out of line but also totally unbelievable. "You're a writer, you know how it is — add a layer to an already great story, make it mean even more. It's one thing for him to know we're getting over our breakups, but if he thought we found something better —"

"He's coming back."

Doug's moving so fast, he almost skids to a stop. He's got a new energy, and I almost want to give Charlotte an *I-told-you-so* look, because my lie totally worked. Either that or —

"You know, he's been thinking about what you said, and The Doug thinks you're right, man, he does need to give moving on a shot." He's talking rapid fire as he fumbles to take his phone out of his pocket. "The Doug does need to put himself back out there, and look what he found in his inbox!" He turns the phone around and shows us an email he's gotten, a garish poster of lots and lots of cartoon couples making out, under the words *"KISS UNDER THE MISTLETOE — Find that special someone this Christmas!"* A kiss fest with strangers? No thanks. "The Doug's been getting this email for weeks, but he never really paid attention until tonight. And to think he was almost gonna set this email as junk." Then he looks at us and asks the question I didn't know I was dreading. "Wanna go?"

Thankfully, Charlotte's on the ball. "But it's a singles' night, Doug." As if to prove her point, she takes my hand. We take a second trying to get our fingers interlaced properly but don't quite manage it. Charlotte's index and middle fingers end up curled in my thumb.

Doug doesn't seem to notice or care. "Come on. Please? I'm not sure I'll have the nerve to go by myself. I'm kind of shy ..."

Man, he's talking in first person — now I *know* he's being genuine. But still, I don't want to go to a singles' night. I'm about to tell him that ladies love shy guys, but Charlotte's telling him that of course we'll go. Apparently, we'd *love* to.

"Oh, that's great, guys, that's great. I owe you."

Doug turns back to the bar to work on finishing his whiskey, while

I turn to Charlotte and motion for her to shuffle back to where we were standing before. I keep my voice to a mumble.

"You sure about this?"

She nods to the book poking out of her tote bag. "Check out Step Seven."

I crouch to retrieve the book, flick through it to the seventh chapter and discover that we're now taking things up a notch: "Hook up with someone new."

~ CHAPTER SEVEN ~

CHARLOTTE

5. *DO SOMETHING FOR SOMEONE WORSE OFF THAN YOU.*

Taking care of someone who needs you teaches you how to maintain your positive energy, but what about when you need to do some emergency patchwork on your heart? Being there for someone else in a time of crisis is one of the best ways to show yourself how strong you really are.

10:10 P.M.

"Can you believe it?" says Doug, his voice worryingly wheezy. "I've never taken a *single* break-dancing class."

I can easily believe that Doug has never taken a single break-dancing class. I don't think he's ever *seen* a break-dancing video. His pop and lock is more lurch and flop, and his attempt at the worm makes me fear for his face, his knees — every bone in his body! I could give him the benefit of the doubt and assume it's hard to break-dance well on a moving 6 train (the carriage has been empty since we got on it at

Grand Central, and I have been *very* grateful for that), but I'm fairly certain it's more that The Doug is simply terrible at this.

For his big finish, he grabs a support pole with one hand, wrapping a leg around it and spinning. I *think* he's going for a 360 — but at about 155 degrees, he loses his grip and goes slamming into the bench seat behind him. Anthony and I have been watching this for nearly three stops, and I can't take it anymore, so I applaud Doug in a way that makes it clear I've assumed it's the end of the performance. Doug half rises off the bench and gives us a little bow.

"Let's see the single ladies of the Upper East Side resist *those* moves," he says, crossing his arms and reclining. I hide my face behind Mistake's head, trying not to snort into her fur.

Moments later, we get off the train at Eighty-Sixth Street station, Doug in the lead. He's taking the stairs two at a time, and it's a struggle to keep up. Once I'm on the street, I realize Anthony's not with me. He's dawdling up the stairs the way my sister Emma does when she disagrees that it's bedtime.

"What's the matter?" I ask him. "You hurt your leg or something?"

"Forgive me for not being super thrilled to set foot on the Upper East Side," he says as he draws level with me.

"Weren't we on the east side earlier?"

"That was *Lower* East Side."

"Still east."

He shakes his head at me. "Wait 'til you've lived here awhile. You'll understand."

He says that like my coming back is a foregone conclusion. I must admit, there have been long stretches of today where I've not hated on New York the same way I had been doing since …

Experiencing it with Anthony *has* made me see it differently.

By 10:25 p.m., Doug has led us to a club called Smooch (which Anthony said was a name "*so* East Side the place might as well be a barge on the East River"). My lack of ID isn't a problem for the bouncer here, either, because he's engrossed in a Sudoku puzzle. He has only one question: are we *sure* we want to go in? When Doug insists we do, the bouncer takes Doug's money — he's paying for all three of us, it seems — and mumbles something about it being our funeral.

The club certainly has a funereal atmosphere inside — it's not quite as dead as Ice Bar, but it's still pretty bleak: dimly lit, the beige walls decorated with the kind of tinsel and Christmas wreaths the Salvation Army wouldn't even accept as donations. The whole scene is made even more absurd by the fact that the music (currently a-ha's "Take On Me") is blaring at eardrum-rattling volume. Mistake wriggles, and I have to shush her before she tries to harmonize with the high notes.

I count maybe a dozen singles, mostly over forty, standing around and staring into space. There are three "couples" in booths over by the far wall, making out like they're on a plane that's about to crash into a mountain. Cheese would be in Heaven here. I can't tell if the people standing are nervous about approaching others, or if they've scouted the options and decided, simply, *no*. What I do know is that they are hugging the walls, keeping well away from the low-hanging mistletoe.

We follow Doug as he drifts over to the bar, scanning the room and nodding. "More ladies than dudes." He sounds so approving, I half expect him to do a fist pump.

"There always are." A woman — about ten years older than Doug, maybe — speaks from the bar, a pink drink in front of her.

I nudge Anthony, point to her glass, whisper: "Look at *that* brolly." He just shakes his head at me — but he smiles. I'm trying to make him laugh, because, I don't know why, it feels important to me. Maybe I'm trying to repay him for how he held me together after Katie's party.

"We have a theme here, as you can see," says Mrs. Pink Drink. I notice a badge with some company's logo pinned to her lapel. Guess she's one of the organizers for this thing. "To leave, you must earn yourself one of these." She holds up a business card that has a bell attached to it. It jingles annoyingly with every move. "This is your Jingle Pass. This alone proves to the bouncer that you're allowed to go."

"How do we 'earn' a" — it seems to take effort for Anthony to say the words — "Jingle Pass?"

"Have one kiss under the mistletoe, while I'm watching. That's all you've got to do."

As Doug gets us drinks — nonalcoholic ciders — Anthony and I turn back to the "prospects."

"Anybody take your fancy?" I ask him.

"Looks like a bookish crowd," he mumbles. "Theoretically, we should fit right in, don't you think?"

"I'm not being funny or anything, but … have you ever kissed an *older* person before? Like, years older?"

"Yeah, once."

I can't help it. I shift and sidestep so that he can see me gawp at him. "Oh my God, really? Who? And how old?"

He smiles again, looks to the floor. "Oh, no, this is a story I take to the grave."

"At least confirm or deny whether she was in the same age bracket as the women here."

"I'm not telling you." He's still grinning, but his face is reddening.

"You're no fun."

Doug's back with the drinks. He's bought another whiskey for himself.

"What are you two talking about?"

"Just who we might approach," I say, without thinking, because of course Doug asks:

"What do you guys need to approach anybody for? You've got each other."

Thank God for Anthony, thinking quickly. "We figured we'd at least mingle a little," he says, gesturing with the bottle at the near empty room. "Moral support."

Doug peers at us for a long moment, and I fear he's seen through our act. But then he starts grinning, almost bouncing on his toes. "This is just what I needed tonight, guys. Seriously, I can't believe I made such good friends."

Anthony claps Doug on the shoulder. "All right, then — let's do this."

7. HOOK UP WITH SOMEONE NEW.

Can't imagine a future without your ex? How can you be sure about tomorrow when you haven't explored all the possible todays?

✴

Within a few minutes, I find myself standing flat against a wall — avoiding the mistletoe — being hit on by Rudolph the Red-Nosed Reindeer. Okay, he's actually a slightly nerdy guy in a burgundy sweater vest with a reindeer sock puppet, but still — he's speaking through "Rudolph," and I'm now so keen to get out of here, I'm wondering whether kissing the sock puppet will get me my Jingle Pass.

"Rudolph thinks your accent is *very beguiling*." Finally, Sweater Vest speaks for himself, but there's something about his tone, his choice of words, that makes my shoulders hunch — and makes Mistake lean up out of my tote bag and growl. Sweater Vest must not have noticed her before, because he takes a step back, but Rudolph is still kind of leaning in — close enough for Mistake to snap her teeth and whip him off the guy's hand.

"No, Mistake!" I yelp, almost dropping my tote bag as I try to save

Rudolph, but I only succeed in tearing him in half. I hand the remains back to Sweater Vest. "I'm so, so sorry."

He takes the pieces of his puppet from me, cradling them in his hands and gasping, "Oh, no, Rudolph ... Sweet, innocent Rudy ..."

He might be trying to be funny, but I am *not* waiting around to confirm this. I move off and run into Anthony, who is backing away from a table with his hands raised in what looks like surrender. When Mistake nuzzles his arm, he uses that as his excuse to turn completely away from the mousy-haired girl — who might be the only twenty-something in here — sitting at the table, flicking through what looks like a travel brochure.

"I think I may have just gone halfsies on a time-share in Myrtle Beach," Anthony mumbles.

"That's nothing," I mumble back. "I got hit on by a sock puppet ... and Mistake kind of murdered him."

He leans down and kisses Mistake's head. "Good girl."

I think about asking Anthony if he wants to get out of here — but when I scan the room and look for The Doug, I see that he's sitting at the bar, deep in conversation with a woman his age, whose violet blouse is open, revealing a blood-red corset underneath. It's too dark in here for me to make out the tattoo on her chest, but I can see that it covers all of her skin. Not whom I would have pegged as Doug's type, but he seems kind of rapt. So I shrug at Anthony.

"Round Two, I guess?"

He looks reluctant, but he nods. "One conversation, one kiss, and then we get out of here? Get far away from the Upper East Side?"

"Deal."

*

"Let me break it down for you, okay?"

It's about five minutes since we began Round Two, and I'm already regretting asking Tag — that's *actually* his name — why he's still wearing his Rand-Paul-for-President T-shirt, even with how the election went down. He didn't think my accent was "beguiling" so much as an invitation to go on (and on and on and *on*) about "big government" and taxes that are too harsh on "job creators" — concepts we Europeans are "stubbornly refusing" to get with, apparently. I'm sure there are Europeans who can make heads and tails of what he's saying, but I don't really understand what he's talking about. Which really doesn't matter, because this is more lecture than conversation. I decide my best course of action is to not say much in response and communicate in "mmms" and "uh-huhs," maybe offer him the occasional "right, right."

As I'm doing this, I'm looking for Anthony, but I can't see him anywhere. Has he got his Jingle Pass? Is he waiting impatiently for me so we can leave? Who might he have kissed?

I'm on autopilot with the wordless responses when the words "next Tuesday" cut through everything like an air horn. I realize that I'm now nodding, but I have absolutely no idea what I'm nodding to — I just know that it's happening next Tuesday.

"Wait, sorry," I say. "Run that by me again?"

"Next Tuesday," says Tag, "I'll take you to the range. You know, let you get comfortable with the Second Amendment." He forms his fingers into guns and actually makes little "pew pew!" sounds as he fires them at the ceiling.

Oh *no*.

There's only one thing for it — it goes against every fiber of my Englishness, but sometimes being blunt and rude is your only option.

"No." I move past Tag. "That is definitely not for me. Goodbye."

I walk off, fighting the urge to apologize. Ohmygodohmygodohmygod, that was so rude, that was so rude. Then I hear Tag calling after me: Do I have a problem with guns? If I do, apparently I ought to watch I don't slip on the mess my bleeding heart has made — "You liberal!"

I stop feeling bad about being rude.

As I'm walking past the door to the gents', Anthony charges past me and pushes his way into it. I think that … was he … *crying*? Oh no, he hasn't had some kind of Maya relapse, has he? He was doing so well!

I quickly scan and make sure that no one's looking my way, so that I can duck into the gents'. I find Anthony hunched over the sink. He sniffs and wipes his eyes. Guess this is how I get to repay him for keeping me together after the party.

I take a hesitant step forward. "Hey, you okay?"

He sniffles. "Yeah, yeah, I'm fine. I just need a minute."

"Might have been a *mistake*" — I hold up my bag, even though he can't see me to appreciate the brilliant pun — "coming here, huh?"

He doesn't answer. He just takes a wet, rasping breath.

"But, seriously, you've been doing great tonight. Don't backslide now, you're going to be fine."

He speaks into the sink, his voice echoing. "What are you talking about?"

"Well, I mean … you're upset about M— *her* again, right?"

He makes no sound, but I see his shoulders juddering. Oh no, I've set him off, and now he's sobbing his heart out. All that work undone.

Then I notice that he's not so much boo-hoo-ing as ha-ha-ing. Is he … *laughing*? He straightens up and turns around — his face is slick with the tears streaming from his eyes, but he's definitely laughing.

"I'm not crying over Maya," he says, leaning forward and putting his hands on his knees. "I just spent Round Two with a girl named Erin — she brought her cats! All three of them. I'm allergic, that's all."

We both start laughing, the sound so loud and echo-y in the gents' that Mistake wakes up and grumbles at us, like, *What's* wrong *with the two of you? I'm trying to sleep!*

The laughter fades away, and we just stare at each other for a few seconds — a weird silence but not all that uncomfortable. "Listen," he says, and his allergic reaction must be passing because his voice is starting to sound less scratchy. "Making Step Seven's going to be tough. Everyone seems nice and all, but … I dunno, there's no one who I'd call my 'type' out there."

"Same. Let's get out of here. I'll tell Doug."

I jump and spin around when the door to the gents' flies open, hitting the wall with a thunderous thud that makes Mistake almost fly out of my tote bag. The first thing I notice is Mrs. Claus — well, a woman dressed like Mrs. Claus — dragging someone into the toilet. It's Doug, and he's grinning like a loon and fake whispering:

"But what if your husband catches us? I'll *never* get off the Naughty List."

Mrs. Claus pulls Doug in closer as the bathroom door closes. "But then you'll be on *my* Naughty List." I guess she's found out about Gee-Gee and is getting back at Santa.

"That sounds like it's much more fu— Hey, guys!" When he sees us, Doug almost shoves Mrs. Claus away from him.

"Hey, Doug …" Anthony's only just keeping it together as he gives Doug's new lady friend a polite bow. "Ma'am."

Mrs. Claus is a rather … buxom woman who looks to be around Doug's age, and I can only assume she needs at least the last three hours of every day to remove her makeup. Where Doug's looking at his shoes, she's just shaking her head — finding this funny more than mortifying. I like that.

I say that Anthony and I are going to take off, and The Doug marches forward to pull both of us into a hug. "This was a great idea, you guys. *So* great! Thank you, thank you, thank you." He kisses us both on the cheek. I could do without the whiskey breath, if I'm honest, but I'm happy for him — and pleased that we crossed off Step Five.

Anthony and I leave them to it, stepping out of the bathroom. We both pretend we don't hear a stall door slamming shut, a lock being thrown across. We just put as much distance between us and the bath-room as we can, walking back to the bar and standing behind Mrs. Pink Drink, who's explaining the rules to two more singles — one man, one woman, both in some kind of comic book–themed T-shirts, looking equally nervous, and I wonder if they're the only two people who don't realize how good they look together.

I turn to Anthony. "Shall we go, then?" I guess I'll complete Step Seven — hook up with someone else — another time. When I'm back home. I mean, it's probably about time I started kissing English boys ...

He nods, and we start toward the exit, only for Mrs. Pink Drink to remind us that we don't have Jingle Passes. "Ah, it's okay," says Anthony. "Thanks, anyway."

Mrs. Pink Drink leans forward on her bar stool, motioning to the thick-necked, burly guy I've only just noticed standing by the front door that he's not to let us out. "I don't think you understand," she tells us. "No one leaves here without earning a Jingle Pass."

Damn it, from where she is sitting, she can see the whole room — so we can't even say that we've just kissed one of the people we'd been talking to. But then, even in Imaginary Land, I don't think I could bear anyone knowing I'd snogged Tag — or Sweater Vest. And Anthony wouldn't have survived a kiss with Erin the Cat Lady.

He's pulling me aside as I ask him, "Can she really stop us from leaving? She can't care that much!"

Anthony's just looking at me, his face saying, *I have no idea.* "There's something about her that tells me she'll give us shit if we try to walk out of here un-kissed."

"Don't tell me you're frightened of making a scene. That's supposed to be a British thing. You lot are supposed to be all American and forth-right and not give a ... What, why are you looking at me like that?"

His face has become very still, his eyes slightly narrowed as if I'm a riddle he's almost solved.

"You know, there is *one* way out of here," he says.

"What's that?"

He just raises his eyebrows at me. I know we've not been apart for, like, the last seven hours or so, but that doesn't mean I've developed the skill to read his …

Oh.

I can't believe I didn't think of it before. Or had I been ignoring the obvious? No — there's no way my cheeks would be burning the way they are right now if I wasn't surprised.

Anthony wants to kiss *me*.

Or does he? I seem to have paused so long, he's changed his mind. "Nah, it's a dumb idea."

"No, it's not. It's just to get us out of here. It's no big deal, right?"

He says nothing — just closes his eyes for a second (working up courage?), then leans in …

And gets a faceful of Mistake, the pup rearing up out of my tote bag, stealing my kiss for herself.

"Get down, you!" I laugh, shoving her back into my bag. When I look back at Anthony, he has one hand over his eyes, and he's shaking his head, like, *Could that have gone* any *worse?*

I know that if I don't laugh along, the moment might pass. So I point out to him that Mrs. Pink Drink wasn't looking anyway and might not have believed us. Also, we're not under mistletoe, and I know she's *that* much of a cow that she'll disqualify us just for that. Imagine *that* scene! So, I move forward and take Anthony's hand, pulling him over to the nearest mistletoe, beside a table where — bloody hell — Tag is chatting up the Tattooed Corset Lady Doug was talking to earlier.

I position us so that we're in Mrs. Pink Drink's line of sight. I make sure she's looking at us, giving her a nod. Then I feel weird for doing so — like she's really invested in this moment or something.

This is it. This is going to happen. I'm now hyper aware of the fact that Anthony's taller than Colin, and I'm going to have to get on my tippy-toes — unless he's going to lean all the way down? When I reflexively lick my lips, I notice that they're a bit dry and chapped from the cold, and I try to figure out how I can ask Anthony for a time-out so I can scrounge up the lip balm in my tote bag when —

He kisses me. It's a little more than the peck that I was expecting — softer, deeper, lingering for maybe three seconds before I feel his hand on my elbow, holding me close as he pulls away. After, I purse my lips so as not to make any embarrassing gasps, but with my racing heart, the quickening breaths I take through my nose quickly make me feel light-headed.

We're looking into each other's eyes, and I think we're both a little stunned by how great the kiss was. Unless, I'm stunned, and *he's* just grossed out by my chapped lips. But he's not making a face, so that's good, right?

We snap out of it at the sound of jingle-jangling coming from over by the bar. Mrs. Pink Drink's holding out our passes. I step forward and take them from her. "I'm glad *someone's* having a good Christmas Eve," she says, and it's now very clear to me that she's not a stickler for any real rules — she just doesn't want to be here. I wonder what her story is, tentatively adding her to the number of lovelorn and heartbroken people Anthony and I met tonight.

"Charlotte."

That's Anthony, and he's motioning at me that we should get going.

"Yes!" Even a full minute later, my voice is still a little high and squeaky, affected by the kiss. His sounds normal.

I follow him out of Smooch, past the bouncer, who doesn't even look up from his Sudoku when Anthony drops the jingling passes next to him.

Anthony leads me a little way down the street, then comes to an abrupt stop in front of me. I just stare at the back of his head, trying to guess at the look on his face. Is he thinking about the kiss? Is he regretting it? He kind of shouldn't — *he* was the one doing all the leaning, after all!

But when he turns around, he's got a smile on his face. He liked it, I know he did. I smile back at him, make a face, like, *I know, right?*

"It's really pretty out now."

I'm thrown. "Huh?"

He takes my hand again, pulls me to him. "Stand here. Look."

It takes me a second to re-center myself and for my eyes to follow where he's pointing. At first, I wonder what the hell he's pointing at. But then I see the twinkle of twirling snow, turning golden as it dances around the streetlights on Eighty-Sixth Street. It's strangely still and peaceful, and this stillness lessens my homesickness somehow. It's so quiet, so pleasant, I'm not feeling the distance. Only the moment.

When I realize that Anthony's still holding my hand, I feel heat rising to my cheeks, feel my arm stiffen against his. He looks down sharply, then pulls away with a mumbled "sorry." I want to tell him there's really no problem, but before I can, he's asking me: "What next?"

What next? I mean, we can go somewhere quiet, if anywhere is open, and maybe talk about what just happened, what it might mean. After I've thought all of this, I realize that he of course means, *What's the next step?*

"Oh!" I let him take Mistake and her leash out of the tote bag, so the little madam can stretch her legs on the sidewalk, while I take out the book again. Only three more steps left, by my count. I find the eighth one and turn the book around so that Anthony can see it: "Do something that scares you a little."

Anthony ponders this, and I know that something has immediately come to his mind. But when I ask him, he just shakes his head. "I think we should focus on you now," he says. "It's your last night, and there's only a few hours left for you to do all the steps. So, what scares *you*, Charlotte?"

5. ~~DO SOMETHING FOR SOMEONE WORSE OFF THAN YOU.~~

7. ~~HOOK UP WITH SOMEONE NEW.~~

~ CHAPTER EIGHT ~

ANTHONY

8. *DO SOMETHING THAT SCARES YOU A LITTLE.*

One of the worst things about finding yourself Suddenly Single is the Fear that comes with it. The Fear of what tomorrow might — or might not — bring, now that your relationship is over. In many people, Fear can cause a kind of emotional and spiritual paralysis that results in them spending too much time at home, at the expense of looking for someone new. Of course, the thought of "getting back out there" is terrifying, and Fear is totally understandable in this situation. Before you can conquer your fear of romantic disappointment, you must first learn to conquer Fear itself ...

11:10 P.M.

"Are you sure this is safe? I mean, is it even *allowed*?"

Charlotte's clinging to my right arm, almost jogging to keep up with me, because I'm walking fast to keep up with Mistake. I should have figured that the pup would get super excited the minute she laid eyes on Central Park. Even after eleven at night, it's pretty amazing — to a dog, it must look like Heaven or something.

All the way here, I did ask myself if this was a good idea. But I couldn't help it. Outside Smooch, after our kiss — the *kiss!* — I asked Charlotte what scared her, and she said the only thing she could think of was being out of control. When I told her that was an unhelpfully vague answer, she just shrugged, but all the snow we were staring at gave me an idea.

"Of course it's safe," I tell her now. "This time of night, on Christmas Eve, we'll have the whole park to ourselves."

"*These* don't look safe," says Charlotte, glancing down at the two Flying Saucer sleds I bought for fifteen bucks at a drugstore on our way here.

I come to a stop. Up ahead, Mistake turns and yaps her annoyance. Charlotte's looking up at me, her hands gripping the straps of the tote bag over one shoulder. She's chewing on her bottom lip, but there's nothing flirtatious about it. She's scared.

"Trust me."

She nods. "Yeah, I trust you."

I hadn't meant it as a question, but I don't correct her. "Okay, good, because we're about to abandon the path." I give Mistake's lead a tug and she turns, bounding ahead as we cut across the snow-covered lawn. Charlotte lets out a nervous laugh. "Um, *where* are you taking me?"

Mistake stops when we come to a row of bushes, looking back at me, like, *Seriously? You want me to go through* that?

"It's okay, sweetie," I call, and as the pup scrabbles through the bushes, I cringe at myself. I'm already calling her pet names. What the hell?

Charlotte uses the sleds to shield her face as we fight our way through the bushes, stopping at a six-foot iron fence. Mistake thinks it's a dead end and tries to run left, so I yank her back and pull her toward us. She lets me know how happy she is about that.

"Have we come the wrong way?" Charlotte asks, as I bend down to pick up the dog.

"Nope," I tell her. "On the other side of this is the best sledding in Manhattan — maybe the whole of New York, I dunno. Me and my brother, Luke, used to come here on Sundays. Our mom brought us here ..." I take a moment to let my mind get used to screening a memory it purposely hasn't thought about in a year. I'm kind of an idiot for not realizing exactly what it was that made me think sledding would be a good step for Charlotte. "I was around seven years old, I think. Anyway, it's not *technically* legal for us to do this, 'cause the land belongs to the parks department. But I gotta think they've taken today off."

She's staring at me, openmouthed. "Hey, that's good," I say. "Looks like you're *definitely* doing something that scares you."

She slaps my arm. "I seriously doubt the book advises breaking the law."

"I'm sure you can interpret the book in lots of different ways. And hey — there's not much scarier than breaking the rules, right? This might be the purest version of Step Eight that's possible to take!"

"I'm a foreigner here, remember? What happens if I, you know, get arrested and deported and can never come back?"

"Hmm, arrested and deported ... sounds *scary*."

"You really want to do this, don't you?"

I only just manage to stop myself from telling the truth: that yes, now that I've realized what, subconsciously, led me here, sledding on the pristine white hills on the other side of this fence feels like the *only* thing I want to do. I want to feel seven years old again, excited and scared as I watched Luke sled fearlessly down the steepest hills, while Mom sat me on her lap and did the sledding herself, then said it was all me once we were at the bottom.

Instead, I tell her: "It'll be fun, I promise. Me and Luke have been sneaking in since we were kids, and we've never been caught — there's got to be even less chance of us getting caught tonight."

She thinks on it for a second, then gives a nod that's not all that reluctant. "Okay, let's do it. But be quick ..."

"Oh, as soon as you hit peak scared, we're out of here."

I hand Mistake to Charlotte so she can put the pup back into her tote bag as I hop the fence. On the other side, I reach up so Charlotte can toss the sleds to me. Then she climbs up high enough to gently swing her bag over the fence so I can take it. I put the sleds down and hang the bag from my shoulder as Charlotte climbs over. She's more agile than I expected.

Once she's safely down, I hand her the bag back. Mistake is craning to see what's up, and I assure Charlotte that this area of the park is totally fenced off. Mistake might run, but she won't get *too* far.

"Okay, good," says Charlotte, letting the dog out. "I don't want to lose her."

We don't have to worry about losing her, because as soon as we take out the sleds and get into position at the top of the first slope, Mistake is all over us, wanting to be exactly where we are. She settles in my lap.

"I guess I've got a passenger." But Charlotte doesn't smile back at me. She's staring down the pure white hill, at the lake of shadow down at the bottom.

"It's a bit steep," she says.

"Yeah, it's scary," I tell her. "That's the point."

"What if I — you wanker!"

She calls me that because I've given her a push. Not a hard one — just hard enough to get her going.

I hold Mistake close and sled down after Charlotte, enjoying the weightless feeling and only just stopping myself from crashing into her. Any fear she had before is gone — she's now lying half off the sled, laughing up at the night sky as the snow falls on her face.

"Hey, hey, not so loud," I tell her, as Mistake jumps off my lap and runs in an arc from one side of Charlotte's head to the other, like a windshield wiper. "It might be deserted, but that just means noise travels."

She claps a hand over her mouth, as she sits up, controlling herself. "Sorry," she says, finally. "Just got a bit of a … rush, I guess. Once the fear passed, I kind of liked it."

"I guess that's the point." I don't mean for this to be anything intense, but the fact that we're staring right at each other when I say it makes the eye contact we hold feel much more significant.

The spell is broken when Mistake yaps for attention, and we see that she's halfway up the hill, looking back, clearly expecting us to follow.

Charlotte prods my toes with hers. "Race you!"

*

About ten minutes later, we've gone up and down the same slope twenty times. After three or four turns, Charlotte got confident enough to try going backwards. She laughed the entire time.

Now, Charlotte's collapsed in a heap at the bottom, lying on her back again as Mistake runs circles around her, while I come charging down backwards, careful to get as close as I can without crashing into her. I can actually steer myself pretty close, and she makes no attempt to move. She trusts me.

I let myself fall next to her, feel the backs of our fingers grazing as we laugh at the night — both of us, I guess, wondering how the hell we've ended up illegally sledding in Central Park on Christmas Eve.

I can hear her laughter's dying down, and all I want to do is look to my left. If I do that, we might have a "moment." But it's like one side of my neck fills with concrete or something, because it just won't move.

"Thank you." Her voice is almost a whisper.

I still can't turn my head. "For what?"

She doesn't answer, and the silence goes on long enough that I know she's waiting for me to look at her. So I take a breath to relax, then finally turn my head. Her long hair is lashed across her face in thick strips, dappled with snow.

"For letting me see it's all right to be scared sometimes."

"New Charlotte's okay with being scared?"

"Yeah, she is ..."

My breathing is shallow, and my arms are quivering — from more than just the cold, I'm sure of that. I think too long about my next move: could I reach across and move the hair from her face with these shaking hands, or would I just poke her in the eye?

And if I got close enough to do that, could I do the thing that I'm now wishing I hadn't stopped doing in Smooch?

Could I kiss her again?

It's all a moot point when Charlotte sits up so quickly that Mistake takes off running, thinking there's more sledding to be done.

"So, what's your thing?" Charlotte asks, moving her hair out of her face. "What scares *you*?"

The answer comes to me right away, and I really don't want to talk about it — but I can't think of anything to say in its place, so I just end up staring at her for a few seconds.

"Uh, you know ..." I dig deep for anything scary. "Sharks, I guess. But I don't have to face my fear ever, because there are no sharks in Brooklyn — well, there are *loan* sharks, if you need one. But I never do, so ..."

Crap, now it's me who's rambling, and Charlotte's looking at me, and I can tell she knows that I'm hiding something. I sit up, grind my fist into the snow and frozen grass. Oh, God, I'm actually going to talk about this. "You really want to know? Even if me telling you might, like, puncture your Christmas spirit?"

She smiles, leans forward. "Have you not been paying attention tonight? Aren't we 'muddling through'?"

"Yeah, I guess we are. Okay … I'll tell you what it is."

And I want to tell her. I really do. But everything I want to say slams up against the lump in my throat, because I'm wondering if my being in Central Park on the sledding slopes on Christmas Eve, about to confide in a random English girl, is somehow meant to be.

If Mom somehow brought me here.

"My, uh, mom …" As if sensing I might need her for this, Mistake literally jumps into my lap, and I automatically hug her to me. "My mom died last year. On Christmas Day."

Charlotte shifts forward, drawing level but still facing me. "Oh, my God, Anthony."

The sympathy in her soft voice is real; the squeeze of her hand on my forearm is genuine. But everything I've been keeping contained for the last year is threatening to come charging out, and that's why I don't talk about it. I never once did with M… with my last girlfriend. Not after the funeral. It was the only way I knew how to keep it together.

And I can't cry in front of Charlotte.

So I lean down and kiss Mistake's head, fussing over the pup until the lump in my throat falls away, until my chest loosens up enough to let more than tiny wisps of air into my lungs, and I feel like I can talk again.

"Cancer," I tell Charlotte, trusting that that single word means I don't have to give any more detail about the type, about the chemo, about what the chemo did to her, about the unthinkable amount of time between the doctor saying there was nothing more they could do and the day she actually died, about how bad it got toward the end …

"I'm so sorry" is all she says. It's all anyone ever really can say.

"That's why I was so stubborn about being at the airport today. I so didn't want to go home that I convinced myself it would be totally cool for me to surprise … *her.* That there's no way she would leave me to face the holidays by myself."

I'll bet the significance of the day for me was totally lost on her, too. That's how little she cared about me.

But I don't say this to Charlotte, because we're past talking about exes.

"Your family might need you, though," she says, sliding her hand into mine.

I can't help scoffing. "They're fine. My aunt Carla basically, like, annexed our kitchen this morning. There's a huge feast happening to-night at the Monteleone house."

"Sounds like it might be nice — family, all together, keeping each other strong."

"It's a goddamned joke!"

The pain in my heart hits me only after I hear the pain in my own voice. A rebel thought has slipped through my defenses, out into the world, and has left behind an ache in my chest and a sting in my eyes. Mistake whines and shifts to stand up in my lap, wagging her tail at me to calm down. "Sorry," I mumble to her and Charlotte. "It's just … I don't get how everyone can just come together like always, like it's a normal Christmas. It's *not* a normal Christmas, and I'm not going to pretend it is. It's not Christmas without her. It won't ever be."

Charlotte says nothing. We just sit in the snow, holding hands, me cuddling Mistake and taking deep breaths, trying to keep it together. I haven't cried since Mom passed — and, I don't know why, but I don't *want* to. I feel like I can't let myself.

She squeezes my hand again. "You need your family. And they need you. I can go with you, if you like? You turning up with a Brit would surely make a great story to tell *next* Christmas."

I squeeze her hand back. "You serious?"

"Why not? I can distract everybody, and then it might not seem such a big deal to *you* to be back home. There's just one thing I have to ask first, though."

"What's that?"

"What type of Brit do you want to bring home tonight? Is my actual voice all right, or should I go more *Downton* for the giggles?"

"I really don't hear much difference."

She makes a mock offended pout. "You cheeky — argh!"

We're both blinded by the blazing spotlight that hits us right in the face, and we release each other's hands to shield our eyes.

"What the —"

"*Freeze! Police!*"

Oh, yeah. I'd forgotten about the trespassing.

~ CHAPTER NINE ~

CHARLOTTE

11:30 P.M.

I have to shield my eyes against the cop's flashlight, which — in the darkness of the park — feels more like a spotlight.

I am going to get arrested! Ohmygodohmygod, I'm going to get arrested and deported, and I will never be allowed back — even if I want to take up my spot at Columbia, I will be turned away by Immigration! I'm going to get to the immigration booth, and some guy with a mustache — I'm seeing a guy with a mustache, I don't know why — is going to look at my passport, check my name on his computer, then peer at me, like:

"Hold up, honey — are you the little lady who got arrested for sledding in Central Park?"

And my left eye is going to twitch — because it always twitches when I prepare to give a dishonest answer — and I'm going to try to say "no," but he's going to cut me off with a shake of his head. He'll hand my passport back to me, and then two bigger guys are going to appear out of nowhere to say, "Miss, you need to come with us."

Before I know it, I'll be on the next flight home … and I just know that they're going to forget my luggage!

I hear Mistake barking unhappily, feel Anthony wriggle and squirm as he blindly tries to keep her under control. Then comes the sound of boots crunching against the snowy grass, and I start to tell myself that trespassing in Central Park isn't exactly the most serious crime, is it? I'm surely not going to miss my flight because I'm in a cell, right?

And they wouldn't *really* deport me for this …?

"Oh no, oh no, oh no." I'm babbling, and Anthony takes my hand again, squeezing it tight. I dare to open my eyes, finally, and see him looking right at me. He's not freaking out at all. In fact, he looks totally calm, if extremely reluctant about something. He passes Mistake to me and then shifts to face the cop, hands up and held out — not surrender, more *Everything's cool.*

"We're sorry, officer."

The cop is a short guy with a smooth, shaven head. He's almost as wide as he is tall, so muscular he looks like he's about to hulk out of his uniform any second.

"You're trespassing," he says, glaring from Anthony to me. "See that humongous iron fence around here? That means *keep out.*"

Anthony holds up his hands, like, *Oh gosh, my bad.* "I'm so sorry," says Anthony. "I should know better — my big brother's a cop. I just … really wanted to show an out-of-towner a cool New York secret, that's all. Guess we got a little carried away. Call it the Christmas spirit." He makes a show of shaking his head.

The cop stares down at Anthony, aiming the flashlight over our heads — lighting us up but not blinding us. "Your brother's a cop, huh?"

Anthony nods politely. "Yeah — Luke Monteleone. He's at the Seventy-Fourth in Brooklyn."

The officer pulls his mouth into a tight line and walks a few feet away. And within a minute, we're not in trouble anymore. The officer gets on his radio thing (identifying himself as Marquez) and asks ... *someone* to confirm that a Luke Monteleone is a cop at the Seventy-Fourth. When the lady with the crackly voice on the other end says yes, Marquez motions for us to stand up.

"All right, listen," he says, clipping the flashlight back onto his belt. "I guess I can forget what I saw here tonight." He looks away from us for a moment, taking in the snow-covered hills. His eyes flicker, and his lips purse. "I get it ... This place, the two of you. You're young, you want to enjoy the night, you want to enjoy each other."

I duck my face behind Mistake, just in case my embarrassment is obvious.

Marquez smiles at us. "That's all cool, kids. But you also gotta play by the rules, okay? You won't be able to enjoy each other" — why does he keep putting it like that? — "if you're locked up, you know what I mean?"

The cop gets on his radio again, asking if any squad cars are close, and the next thing I know, he's leading us to Fifth Avenue, where a cruiser is pulling up. Officer Marquez approaches the driver's side window. I can see a short-haired woman and curly-haired guy, both in uniform. "Hey, Lainey." I assume her name is actually Elaine. "Thanks for this."

"Wait, what?" I yelp. "You're actually going to arrest us?" I think about running, but I'm not sure I'd get very far carrying Mistake.

Anthony takes a hold of my hand. "It's just a ride home," he mumbles. Then, to Marquez: "I really appreciate it, officer, but we're fine."

Officer Marquez shakes his head. "Kid, I don't know why you'd rather be in the park tonight, but you should get home. It's Christmas. Take it from someone who's not with his family tonight — it's where you want to be."

Anthony stares at the cop for a second, and when I look at him, I can tell that he's biting back protests. He looks at the ground, then at me. "Guess I'm not getting out of Step Eight, huh?"

*

The way Lainey speeds downtown, I feel like *I* could make it home by … all right, not midnight tonight, but definitely before breakfast tomorrow. It helps that while it might not actually be *sleeping*, New York is kind of nodding off as Christmas Eve reaches out for Christmas Day. The streets are silent and so deserted that the sound of Lainey's engine is almost deafening — the whole thing is cooler than I'd ever admit, except for how much it agitates Mistake, whose whine and howl sound like a plea to me and Anthony to *make it stop*!

I turn and face him. "So … your brother grew up to be a cop, then?"

He's looking down at his knees, and when I see his lips curl, I know this is a topic he doesn't really like talking about. "Yeah," he says, shooting a look at Lainey. She's talking to her partner. Neither of them are paying attention to us. "It's only ever useful to me at times like this."

I nudge his arm. "Oh yeah? You take a lot of girls sledding in the park?" He doesn't answer, just shakes his head, like, *Never mind.* "Must be cool to have a policeman brother, though."

Anthony doesn't just laugh — he actually makes a sound like *pah*! "Being the kid brother of a beat cop is … well, let's just say, when you have a brother like Luke — doing the things that he's doing for a living — sitting at home, scribbling in your notebook all day, is not a good look."

"What do you mean?"

"I mean …" He catches himself, then sighs as if to say, *Okay, I'll tell you. Why not?* "My old man never went to college, so he doesn't really know what it's about. Where we come from, people understand how to 'get by,' but they don't really do any planning for the future.

Know what I mean? That's what he's always saying to me, anyway ..."
His voice changes to a low, rasping rumble. "'Anthony, son, what's the
point in preparing to fight tomorrow when today could just come up
and — boom — punch you right in the face?'"

"But you got into Columbia" — just like me — "so surely he ap-
preciates that you've probably got some talent, that you're not wasting
your time?"

"Oh, he gets it," says Anthony, reaching and taking Mistake from
me. The pup sleeps through the movement. "And don't get me wrong,
he is proud. He doesn't know why I want to do it, but he does tell me
that he thinks it's great I can write stories, that I have an imagination.
But" — he switches back into his dad's voice — "'You can't imagine a
future and bring that to life, kid. If we could do that, I'd have grown
up to become shortstop for the Mets.'"

I understand everything but that last sentence!

Anthony smiles, rubs his neck like his Dad impression gave him a
sore throat. "He puts fliers for the Corrections Officer Exam under my
door every other week. Did you know the starting salary can sometimes be thirty grand a year?"

"I did not," I answer, trying to keep my voice light so that whatever's boiling up inside him about his dad doesn't turn to actual anger.
Lainey's now charging into the Battery Tunnel, which, the signs say,
will take us to Brooklyn. Once we're inside, the silence is so heavy, I
feel momentarily deaf. "I'm sure he'll change his tune if you make a
real career out of writing."

"I don't think my dad'll ever really 'get' it. My mom, though, she
... she always liked my stories." He gives a soft smile, and I watch him
for a moment to make sure he isn't going to cry. I'm on the verge of
reaching for him when he shakes his head and looks at me. "So, you
said Columbia, but I didn't ask — what would you study?"

"Journalism. That's always been my dream." I'm suddenly bashful

— I don't often talk about my hopes and ambitions, what I want to achieve, with people. I try not to make it seem like *I* think it's a big deal.

"Cool," he says. "Columbia's journalism program is one of the best in the northeast. Maybe the country."

"Yeah, that's what I've been told, but ..."

I can feel him looking at me. "But what?"

Come on, Charlotte — if he can be honest with you about everything to do with his mum, you can spit this out. "Honestly, I've been thinking that I probably won't take the place."

"You serious? Did you not hear what I just said about how great Columbia's —"

"Yeah, yeah, I heard you ..." I try to look up at him, but it's like an invisible and very heavy hand is keeping my head in place, forcing me to look at my knees. "I knew that ..."

He makes a sound that's part shock, part scoff. "Is it because of Co... him? Some d-bag from Westchester? What is it — did he get early admission, too, and you don't want to have to see him?"

I wish it was that simple. That understandable.

I reach out and scratch Mistake behind the ear, as if I need to draw the courage to keep speaking from her. "No, no, he's deferring college for a year to go traveling. But me, I ... I dunno, New York just looks *different* to me now. I'm not *as* sure as I used to be about moving here."

When he says nothing, I get the sense that he's waiting for me to look at him. I force myself to. The lights of the tunnel pass over his face, so that his gaze is interrupted, flickering. Like the mirror in Macy's, the effect makes the eye contact somehow more intense than normal.

"It's your dream," he says. "The city looks different now? Okay, fine — adjust. It's *your* dream." He takes my hand again, squeezes it once. "You can do it."

Lainey charges out of the tunnel, the flickering shadows gone, leaving just uninterrupted eye contact. After a second, Anthony's cheeks twitch and he looks forward.

"Hey," he says, pointing at the clock on the dashboard. It says 11:59. "It's nearly —"

The clock turns to midnight. We look back at each other, and I'm struck by how ... *normal* this feels, to be in a strange car in a strange city with some boy I've known for about nine hours or so. I really don't know what to do or say in this situation, and it feels okay somehow, and I've no idea why. Maybe because, unlike with *him*, I don't feel a need to "perform" with Anthony, to be something or someone I think he wants me to be. I've let him see all my good sides and some of the not-so-good, and he hasn't run off yet. So, yeah — maybe there's nothing to say right now, and that's okay.

"Merry Christmas." I can barely hear his whisper over the roar of Lainey's engine, and I'm just grateful that the siren isn't on. More than that, I'm thankful that I'm not where I'm supposed to be right now — probably asleep on a plane as it starts to make a descent into London Heathrow. I am no longer upset about my flight being canceled.

Yeah, because that's the thing to focus on right now, Charlotte. Say it back!

But before I can, Anthony turns away, looking forward. I'm still holding his hand, so I squeeze it again.

We sit in silence for a minute or two until Lainey — whose voice rises easily above the roaring engine — calls back and asks where we want to be dropped off. Anthony gives directions to his house, and within five minutes of coming out of the tunnel, we're pulling up to it. We thank Lainey, who tells us to stay out of trouble — and also asks Anthony to tell his brother to call her — and then get out. As the cruiser turns around and drives off, back to the city, we face a simple semi-detached house with a small patch of lawn for a front garden.

The grass is a bit tangled, overgrown, but the potted plants lining the edges tell me that it *used* to be well-tended. I wonder if this was Anthony's mum's pet project. He's kind of crushing my hand, and when I look at him, I see that his jaw is clenched, his lips pursed.

"Remember," I tell him. "If it gets too much, just throw the British girl in front of you as a distraction." Mistake gives a single bark, wriggling in his arms. We both laugh. "Or just chuck this one at the nearest relative."

He smiles for what feels like the first time since we were sledding. "I don't think even Mistake could deal with *that* much fussing."

But he holds her up almost like a shield as he leads me up the steps to the front door. He uses a key to open it, and a second later all I'm aware of is meatballs and murmuring. The sounds and smells are like a strangely pleasant slap in the face, the heat of what's been cooked like a cozy hug, which is a real relief from the cold outside. Anthony leads me into a wood-paneled hallway that seems almost stubbornly old-fashioned, just like the soft, paisley carpet. We have to sidestep right to get past the huge mound of coats and jackets piled on top of each other on the coatrack.

I follow him to the kitchen at the back of the house — five people are sitting at a table, empty plates orbiting pots and casserole dishes, wineglasses and beer bottles in front of them. I wonder how long they've been sitting here after finishing dinner — whether the kitchen has taken on some kind of safe, comforting space for them on this anniversary?

"Well, isn't this cozy?" says Anthony, throwing up his free hand in mock outrage. "The family that eats together!"

At the head of the table is an elderly lady in a dark-green cardigan, who seems powerful and commanding, even though she can't be taller than five feet. On either side of her are two men who look to be pushing fifty (and fifty might be scared to push back). They both have dark hair dappled with gray and flecks of what might be sawdust or paint. I think it's kind of nice that they might be brothers who work together; it must have sucked for them to have to work on Christmas Eve.

But I guess they probably wanted to keep their minds busy today …

The old lady motions for Anthony to sit down and speaks in an accent that wavers between Brooklyn and … somewhere in Italy.

"There's still lots left, Antonio," she says, gesturing to the pots and casserole dishes. "You must be hungry. You've been gone all day."

"Yeah, where you been?" says the man to her right. Anthony's impression of his father really was dead-on. Everyone at the table looks at Anthony. A tall, broad-shouldered guy in a plain white button-down (the youngest in the kitchen, apart from us, so I figure he's Luke the Cop), the other fifty-ish guy, the old lady and a short, slender woman in a brown cardigan and gingham skirt all look at him with concern.

"Everything okay?" Luke asks, draining the last of his beer.

"Yeah, yeah," says Anthony, "it's all good." He does a quick round of introductions for my benefit. The old lady is his grandmother, Fiorella; to her right is his dad, Tommy; to her left is Uncle Frank; the lady in the brown cardigan is Aunt Carla, who I gather is responsible for the feast. Anthony introduces Luke as his "big brother, the cop," and I notice that everyone beams at that, especially Tommy.

Then Luke gestures to Mistake. "What's with the dog?"

"Long story," says Anthony. That's an overstatement, actually, but I don't jump in.

Fiorella is fumbling to put on a pair of Coke-bottle glasses, leaning forward to stare at me over the table. "This your new girlfriend?" she asks Anthony.

"No, Grandma, Charlotte's just a new friend I made tonight," Anthony says. A little quickly.

The old lady looks back to me. "You sick?"

I *think* she's asking me a question, but it sounds more like an assessment. "No, no," I insist. "I'm fine."

"But you're so *pale*," she says, gesturing to the food on the table. "Eat something, immediately!"

I can't help the hand that goes reflexively to my face — my very *pale* face. I just mumble a "thanks" as Anthony sits down at the only empty chair, while Luke gets up and moves to stand by the sink, gesturing for me to sit in his seat, next to Carla, who is already ladling linguini onto plates.

She sets one in front of me, then hands the other to Anthony, who keeps a *very* interested Mistake braced against his chest.

"Give her to me," says Tommy. "I'll let you two eat."

Anthony stands up to hand the pup to his father, Mistake's legs wheeling in the air the whole time. Everyone laughs — except Grandma Fiorella, who slaps the table and insists that someone give the poor dog some food!

Carla's on it, scooping some sausage onto a small plate for Mistake, which she puts under the table. Anthony and I sprinkle some parmesan onto our pasta. I take my first mouthful and try not to react — but it's kind of hard.

"Oh, it's cold, isn't it?" says Carla, reaching for our plates. "Let me heat them up for you."

"No, no, it's fine," I tell her. "Really."

Beside me, Anthony nods and jokes that he likes his pasta "*dead* cold."

Carla looks momentarily mortified, but then she laughs, and so does everyone else, and I know instantly that Anthony's family disproves another idea British people have about Americans — that they don't wind each other up out of affection.

The laughter lasts for about three seconds, the "ha-has" becoming "mmm-mms," which become "mmms," and then everything is silent.

I look down at my food, fearful that if I look up, they'll know I'm trying to figure out how long they've been sitting here tonight.

That I've been told enough to know *why* they might all be sitting in silence. I don't know this family, but I can tell that they don't really want to talk about their grief, which must be worse than usual because it's about fifteen minutes into the first anniversary of losing a mother, wife and sister …

I try to bring the laughter back. "I love how you take the piss out of each other."

Six blank faces stare at me around the table. I can actually imagine Mistake, underneath the table, stopping what she's doing and giving me the same look. Of course — Americans don't really have *that* phrase. To them, I've just called them a family of catheters or something.

"This might be the strangest girl you've ever brought home, dude," says Luke, crossing to the fridge and pointing to his dad. Tommy nods, and Luke gets them both new beers.

Then Luke turns to Anthony. "So, dare I ask?"

"I'd prefer you didn't," says Anthony, through a mouthful of pasta. I feel a soft little lump barrel against my legs. I look down to see Mistake, licking her muzzle and looking up at me like Oliver Twist, asking for more.

"Come on," says Luke, in between swigs. "You were all excited about Maya coming home from college today, and tonight you turn up here with somebody else?"

"Charlotte's a friend," Anthony says again. Like they didn't get that before!

"Something's up," Luke says. He's got a challenging look on his face, matched by all the other grown-ups in the room. "What happened? She come back from Cali with a new boyfriend?"

Anthony doesn't answer, but the pause he takes and the way his shoulders hunch around his jaw is a dead giveaway.

"Oh, you've got to be kidding me," Luke groans, while Fiorella swats at the air.

"I should teach that girl a lesson myself!" Her voice is a snarl, and I look away to hide my grin — I like Anthony's nan.

The family makes sympathetic noises to Anthony, which he waves away. "I'm fine, really," he says, then goes back to eating.

Tommy is shaking his head. "To do that to a boy — today of all days ..."

Silence falls over the table like a giant blanket, and I don't need to look up from my plate to know that no one is making eye contact. My heart squeezes for a non–Love Life reason when I think about how this family is trying to get past their grief, but can't escape talking about the reason they're grieving.

But then Luke snorts. "Well, look on the bright side, man — hold on to whatever gifts you bought, and you can give them to next year's girlfriend. Free Christmas!"

Anthony rolls his eyes. "Stop trying to turn me into a cheapskate. I'm not joining your team."

Luke holds up his hands, laughing for a second, then growing serious. "But you're okay, though?"

Anthony just smiles down into his cold pasta, then looks up and nods. "Yeah. I'm good."

"She won't be," mutters Fiorella. "Not if I ever run into her on the street."

Anthony reaches across the table and squeezes his grandmother's hand. "Let it go, Grandma. I'm good. I promise."

Another silence falls over the table — this one a little less uncomfortable, a little less heavy, than the last.

Finally, Carla mumbles, "Where is that girl? She should come in and say hello. Diana!" Her voice is so loud, I have to lean away from her to save my eardrum. Mistake gives a startled whine from underneath the table. Tommy reaches down to fuss over her and tell her it's okay.

A waifish tween tomboy comes into the kitchen. She's wearing an oversized T-shirt for some band I've never heard of — God, that makes me feel old — and she's got a wide-eyed look about her that's asking the table, *What* could I have possibly done to get in trouble from another room?

"Say hello to Charlotte," says Fiorella. "Anthony's new pale girlfriend."

"No, she's not," says Anthony. A bit quick, making me wonder again if I'm somehow unthinkable. And I hate to admit it, but I wonder if he didn't enjoy our smooch in Smooch as much as I did.

"Hey," Diana says to me.

"Hello, nice to meet you," I say back.

Diana is just making to leave, but she stops mid-turn. "Oh, cool — you're British."

Tommy is grinning at me. "Yeah, you sound like someone off that TV show," he says, snapping his fingers, trying to remember which one. "The one about the family where everyone's marrying their cousin."

"*Downton Abbey*," Fiorella says, swatting the air again as Diana disappears. That appears to be her go-to gesture for everything.

"Yeah, *Downton Abbey*," says Tommy, picking up Mistake and setting her in his lap. "You sound like those guys."

I guess Anthony wasn't kidding when he said it's tough to tell the difference between English regions. And while Tommy is only the second person tonight to say I sound like I belong on *Downton Abbey*, it is starting to grate. I'm from Hampstead, which is at least five rungs down on the Poshness Ladder, I'll have them know!

Mistake is wriggling in Tommy's hands, leaning and stretching for the table.

"Stop it, Mistake," I say. "You've been fed."

She looks at me with, well, puppy-dog eyes, as if to say: *But, Mum, there's so much food. Why* isn't *it for me?*

Carla just smiles, bending down to scoop up Mistake's little plate. "You get one more," she says, "and then you're done, you hear me?"

She scoops up some more sausage and sets it back down. If Tommy didn't have a strong grip on her, I think Mistake might have given herself a concussion diving down for the plate. She goes after her seconds greedily, losing control of the plate a couple of times, sending it sliding along the floor and knocking into table legs.

"God, I hope she calms down soon," Anthony says, helping himself. "It'll be hard to find her a new home if she's this rowdy all the time."

Luke is bending down to fuss over Mistake. His head shoots up sharply. "You can't give her away!"

"Well, are you gonna walk her twice a day?" Anthony asks. "You going to have time between your shifts for that?"

I look at him, trying to figure out what he means. Is he saying that Mistake would be a burden, an inconvenience? I know we haven't had her that long, but I would have expected that she would have meant more to him, like she means to me — because I'm starting to think that one of the reasons I've not thought much about my canceled flight, about getting home, in the last little while is because of that little dog. The dog that feels like *our* dog.

And if Anthony adopted her, then I'd have a chance at seeing her again.

If I come back, that is.

But maybe that's not what he wants?

Fiorella gives a loud tut. "Isabella would have slapped you upside the head if you tried to abandon someone who needs you. Is that how you were brought up, Antonio?"

A hush falls over the table, and I get the feeling that everyone has been waiting for someone to make them all think about who's not here tonight. And now, Fiorella's finally done it. Everyone but me looks down. Luke makes a point of fussing over Mistake.

Tommy clears his throat, leaning a meaty, tattooed forearm on the table. "We'll figure it out," he says.

Carla nods. "We always do."

It's all I can do not to audibly catch my breath, to ignore the prickle I feel in my eyes. Anthony had it wrong earlier, in the park — no one here is pretending that tonight is no different from any other Christmas. Everyone around this table — tight-faced, narrow-eyed, ashen — feels Anthony's mother's absence (hell, even me — and I will never meet her). They're trying to figure out, what do they do *now*?

I'm afraid that if I stare too long, what I'm thinking will become clear. I also worry that if I make eye contact with Anthony, I might start crying for him, so I just look down at my food.

"She has a good appetite." Fiorella nods at Anthony, as if approving his choice of dinner guest.

I feel a tap on my shoulder and turn to look at Carla. Her deep brown eyes glisten with tears she's trying not to release, and I know that she just wants to keep herself occupied. "So, Charlotte, you live here now?"

"Not yet," says Anthony. I shoot him a look: (a) don't answer for me, and (b) we've been talking a lot about this topic tonight, and the one thing I haven't done is make an actual decision.

"I've been on a student exchange program for this semester," I explain. "Getting a feel for what it's like here before deciding whether or not I'm going to come back next year for college."

Carla gets up and goes to the cupboard, taking out a bottle of wine. "You haven't made up your mind?" She holds up the bottle, asking me if I want any.

I shake my head. "It's a big step to take."

"But it's your education," says Carla, pouring a big glass for Frank.

Something about the way she does it — automatic, almost robotic, as if she does this multiple times a day, every day — and the way that she has the same sharp nose as Tommy, sloping slightly left, fills in for me that Carla is married to Frank, and that she's Tommy's sister.

Carla notices me looking. "What?"

"No, nothing," I say. "I've just been trying to figure out who's married to who, but I see now that you and Tommy are definitely siblings."

"Can't escape her," Tommy jokes.

Carla sits back down and pours a drink for herself. "You should give it everything," she tells me. "And Columbia is an excellent school. Isn't that right, Anthony?"

"I like it" is all he says.

Carla goes on: "You need to make the most of your youth — chase your dreams while you've still got the energy to do it."

"You chase your dreams," Tommy mumbles, "you might pull a hammy, means you can't walk too good when you're older. If she doesn't want to risk it, don't be too hard on the girl."

Carla rolls her eyes at him. "It's true — most dreams don't come true, not for most people. But at least you'll be able to say you went after them. Isabella, she … she understood that."

Another hush falls over the table, this one feeling heavier than the last, coming so soon after it. Tommy's voice is the one that breaks the silence as he whispers: "Yeah, she did. She did."

I remember how Anthony was in the first half of our time together — coiled and wound up about things that weren't just to do with Maya; not wanting to go home. He wasn't bottling everything up — he was afraid to talk about it. Because talking about it equals facing up to it, and facing up to it means reliving the grief of losing a mother, a wife, a sister-in-law … The goal of grieving is to get back to normal, but Isabella was clearly such a big part of this family that none of them are sure what "normal" is going to be now.

"I'm so sorry for your loss."

They all look up, faces slack, eyes darting left and right. Lips clamping together as if they don't trust themselves not to start crying. Tommy and Luke nod, acknowledging. Frank looks at the ceiling, lightly shaking his head. Anthony looks at me, and I have to force myself to hold his gaze because I'm suddenly worried I've said totally the wrong thing.

"You're a nice girl." That's Carla again, a thin — but genuine — smile on her face. Then she shakes her head. "Cancer's a terrible thing. But you've got to keep going, right?" Then she smiles at me, in a way that tells me that's as much as they need — or want — to talk about right now. "So, what's wrong with you, Charlotte? You get this great opportunity, and you want to turn it down?"

"It's not that," I say. "I've just … been given a lot to think about."

Fiorella snorts. "That sounds like boy trouble to me."

I say nothing, just stare down at my cold pasta, wondering how I managed to eat so much of it already.

"Let me give you the advice I wish someone had given me when I was your age." I look back up at Carla and can tell that whatever she's about to say next must be deadly serious — she's put down her knife and fork. "Never make a big decision based on where a man fits into it. A woman is only a woman when she is thinking for herself, doing for herself. And most men aren't worth your tears, anyway."

I try not to do it. I try to keep my eyes focused on Carla's. But it's no good. They flit to Anthony, just for a split second.

"Well," says Carla, going back to eating, another gentle smile playing on her lips. "A few of them might be." Then she looks to Anthony. "I'm glad you brought Charlotte instead of that other one. She was pretty, but she was so full of herself, too."

*

After I've eaten, I take Mistake out into the backyard, letting her run around — and do some business — while the Monteleone family winds down inside. The light from the kitchen illuminates a little bit of the backyard — like the front, it is unkempt, wild — and I give Anthony, visible through a window, a wave. He's standing next to Carla, washing dishes that she then dries. As the table was being cleared, Carla asked who'd help. Everyone muttered their offers, and Carla chose Anthony because "he's the only one who's any good."

"Hey, there." Luke comes out into the backyard, another beer in hand. I've been here less than half an hour, and I think that's his third.

Hope he's not on shift tomorrow.

His eyes are as wide as his smile. "So, how is your first experience of an American Christmas?"

I look at Luke, but I can see Anthony's shape in the window, and for some reason, it makes me conscious of how I act around Luke. "It was great," I say. "Although, I don't know how you're all going to get to sleep tonight with bellies full of spaghetti."

Luke grins at me, holds up his beer as an answer. I smile back at him — as briefly as I can. "Well," he says, "I don't think it'll take you all that long to get used to it. You'll have a New Yorker's palate by your midterms."

"Well, that's if I take up the spot at Columbia," I point out.

Luke rolls his eyes at me. "You can't turn it down. It's too great an opportunity. Besides, New York could do with more classy British girls on college campuses."

"Shouldn't we get going?"

Anthony appears at the back door, and while his expression isn't the dead-eyed, don't-mess-with-me look he gave what's-his-name back at the party, I can still tell that he doesn't like what he's seeing. Luke turns to look at his brother, so I feel free to give Anthony a full-on *What-are-you-on-about?* look. It's after midnight, and it's bloody cold.

To be quite honest, I'd be happy to hang out in this warm house, have some more of Carla's delicious food and stay awake until I have to get to the airport.

But Anthony looks like he really does want to go, so I turn and call for Mistake, who comes bounding out of the shadows.

I'll say one thing for that dog — she might be loud, wriggly and *always hungry* — but she learned her name ridiculously quickly. (Maybe she's some kind of dog-genius!) I pick her up and follow Anthony inside, as he ducks his head into the living room and announces that we're going.

The rest of the Monteleone clan thinks we're totally crazy for heading back out so late. Tommy asks why the hell anyone would want to go wandering around when it's nearly one o'clock in the morning.

Anthony holds up his hands in surrender. "Charlotte needs to be getting back to the airport."

I do?

"Oh, Anthony," Carla is standing up from the sofa, disentangling her fingers from Frank's. "I've got something for you. Follow me."

They disappear upstairs for two minutes, and when they come back down, Anthony is carrying a canvas tote bag that has a thick flannel blanket inside.

"It was his old dog's favorite," Carla explains.

"Yeah, it was Max's," Anthony says, and I think his grin is from the memories playing in his mind. "I forgot this was here."

We put Mistake in the bag and say our goodbyes. I collect my tote bag, hook it over my wrist, while Anthony carries Mistake. We go outside and almost become ice sculptures.

"Um, where are we going?" I ask, clenching my jaw to keep from chipping one of my chattering teeth. "Not really the airport? I've still got hours before my flight." What I don't ask: Does he want me to leave?

Anthony points at the tote bag. "You tell me."

Right. The last step. I can't believe we actually ended up doing the whole book!

I take it out, flick to the chapter I need. "Well, according to Dr. Lynch, all we have left is, 'Do something to help yourself gain perspective.' And I suppose, after that, we'll be over ... them." I throw in an incredulous chuckle, but Anthony looks as serious as when he was in the garden just now.

"Pretty vague, no?"

He's right. Perspective. How to gain it?

Before I can talk myself out of the idea I've just had, I grab Anthony's hand. I feel a thrill of excitement when he squeezes it back, our fingers interlacing perfectly this time. "Nearest subway station, now!"

8. DO SOMETHING THAT SCARES YOU A LITTLE.

~ CHAPTER TEN ~

ANTHONY

10. *DO SOMETHING TO HELP YOURSELF GAIN PERSPECTIVE.*

When you're in a relationship, it's very easy for your focus to become narrow, limited only to the Now — the partner in front of you, and what you're doing today. But every step you've taken on this new journey toward a new You has been to get you ready for What's Next. This final step brings all of the previous nine together — you must gift yourself the time and the space to look at the journey you've taken. Only by doing this will you give yourself the confidence to believe that, yes, you will go far tomorrow.

12:55 A.M.

One of the rare benefits of it being Christmas Eve — well, Christmas Day now — in New York is that there's a lot of drunk people on the subway, causing delays and station closures, which means trains skip stops here and there, and the Bensonhurst to Manhattan journey is much quicker than usual. We pass the Broadway–Lafayette Street station after being on the train for only fifteen minutes. Charlotte's head shifts on my shoulder, and I get a mouthful of hair. Then a faceful of Mistake, who's in the tote bag on the seat on my other side. She comes to me as I lean away, stretching up and licking the tip of my nose. Charlotte had better not be asleep, because I don't actually know where she wants to go. On the way to the subway station and as we went through the turnstiles and as we got on the D train, I asked her, "So, where you taking me?"

Each time, she said, "You'll see."

That would usually be the type of thing that totally annoys me. But each time she gave her evasive answer, she'd smile, and I'd just find myself smiling back.

And now I'm remembering what Aunt Carla said as we fetched Max's tote bag from upstairs.

"You've lucked out there, sweetie," she said, rummaging through the closet in my parents' bedroom. Mom's untouched-in-a-year closet.

"What do you mean?" I asked, even though I kind of had an idea what she was talking about. That was the only way to explain why I was feeling *relieved* — relieved that someone else was saying it before I'd said it out loud, proving to me that I wasn't crazy, wasn't getting ahead of myself.

"A keeper has literally wandered into your life," she said, smiling and shaking her head at me, like I was just not getting it. "That girl downstairs is pretty great."

I could feel the smile splitting my face at the same time as my insides swirled and churned. All at once, I was excited that Carla saw it, too, and almost sick with uncertainty. Because there was a time when I had been absolutely sure that Maya and I were for Forever — but Forever lasted just over a year and ended at JFK Airport. If there's one thing that today has taught me, it's that I don't know what the hell a girl is thinking, ever. The only thing I do know right now is that Charlotte is another girl who's going to run away from me this Christmas. Okay, she was always going to do that, because, you know, England, her life there, her family and everything — but still. Girls don't tend to stick around where I am concerned.

That feeling was back — that feeling like I had swallowed glass and it was now lodged in my chest.

"Take your chance to move on," Aunt Carla said, as she was standing up from the closet, carefully replacing the folded clothes she had moved to get at the tote bag. Everything went back in exactly the same spot, as if it had never been moved — as if nothing had changed. Not a lot of "moving on" happening in our family.

"She's going home in a few hours," I said. "And she's not sure that she wants to come back."

"She'll come back," Carla said, handing me the tote bag. "She'll have that whole plane ride to think about it, and by the time she lands, she'll be sure that she wants to come back. But she'll get there only if she *knows* there is something for her to come back to. So, you need to let her know."

As I'm remembering what Carla said to me, I rest my head on Charlotte's, the lilac scent of her hair giving me a little bit of a head rush. It's nice to be close to someone, and for that closeness to be as relaxed and feel as natural as it does with Charlotte. Carla told me to let her know, but what if it's not what she wants? I mean, she hasn't really shown interest in me, has she? It didn't even occur to her that we could kiss each other at Smooch, until I pointed it out, and then she kind of freaked out before she said yeah, okay. And she hasn't mentioned it since. And she might definitely maybe have been flirting with my big brother out in the backyard just before we left.

I tell myself, I could end all this confusion if I just ask her what she wants, what she feels. But how am I going to ask her? Am I going to do it here, on the D train? There's a drunk yuppie lying sideways on the seat opposite us, talking in his sleep about ... something to do with stocks, I don't even know. Am I going to do it at the airport, before she leaves (for possibly forever)? What good will that do?

It will let her know there's something to come back to — that there was always more to New York than that hipster doofus.

Besides, you won't know what she feels if you don't ask her. So, ask ...

But there's one thing I have to ask before that. I hate myself for not being able to help asking it, but I just can't not ask.

"Hey," I say, gently lifting the shoulder she's resting on. She looks up at me through the hair that has fallen over her face, and I have to stop myself from reaching out to move it. That might come with the question after this one. "What were you and Luke talking about, out in the yard?"

"Nothing much," she says instantly — no sign that she's wondering why I'm asking. "I think he was just being a wind-up merchant, that's all."

Great — like *this* is the time for me to need subtitles.

She sees the look on my face and clarifies, speaking through a yawn: "I think your version is, he was 'jerking you around.' Is that it? He wasn't interested in me, he just wanted to make you a bit jealous, to see if you'd throw a fit." She drops her head back on my shoulder. Yawns again. "That's what you two do to each other, innit?"

One hour at my house, and she picked that up. Maya had one year with me, and she'd never gotten there. She always flirted back. It was attention that was being offered, and she could never turn it down. Even if it totally embarrassed me in front of my own family.

Come on, man. Charlotte gets it; she gets you.

Just say it.

"Well, Luke was always good at making me mad." I don't lean my head on hers again, because the way my heart is hammering, I think

I'd give her a bruise. "And he knew for damn sure it'd work tonight, because ... well, I guess he was onto something. I, uh ... I ..." Man, why is this so hard to do?

"I ... had something to get mad about. If you'd asked me this afternoon, could I ever be happy again, I'd have probably laughed at you. Because I don't think I've ever felt less of myself than I did after ... after what happened at the airport. But a few hours with you was all I needed to get better. That's amazing to me. I don't have a clue where this is going, I'll be honest. But I just ... I remember watching you ride off on that Citi Bike, after we'd been at John's, wondering if this night could get any more random than it already had at that point and thinking ... 'I want to find out.' That's how I'm feeling now. I know there is something here today. Tomorrow, the future ...?

"I want to find out."

So much for "just saying it" — I haven't just danced around my point, I've moonwalked and Gangnam Styled. Probably, the only thing I've actually done is put her back to sleep, talking so much.

"I knew you loved me" — there is no pause between the words, but time seems to slow down just for me, so that I can feel the happy swell in my chest, before my gut gets a head start on the churning as I figure out exactly what's coming next — "Colin."

Then her voice, her breathing, collapses to a snore. She's asleep — has been asleep for a while, probably — and she's dreaming about her ex: the guy who broke her heart, who humiliated her at that party.

I'm right here in front of her, and she's still pining for *him*. Even in her alternate dimension, her parallel reality, Colin is still Colin, and she still loves him.

Once again, I feel like I've swallowed glass, only — this time — I also feel like I'm about to throw it back up.

I'm such an *idiot* for not seeing that she wouldn't be over it. She was considering abandoning her dreams, because she couldn't bear to be in the same country as the guy who decided he no longer wanted her. I'm also an idiot for thinking, just now, that there had been no sign that she actually liked me and still choosing to ignore that. I'm nothing more to Charlotte than a jackass from Brooklyn who decided he'd run alongside her, wherever she was going, because, like an idiot, he wanted to "find out."

I sit and stew all the way to the West Fourth Street station, mentally calling myself some R-rated names, when the announcements wake up Charlotte. She rubs her face, tucks her hair behind her ears. "Where are we?"

"West Fourth Street," I say, keeping my voice level, casual. The voice of someone who isn't really all that bothered. "You know what? If you're falling asleep, maybe we oughta skip the last step."

"What? No. I want to keep —"

"You're tired." I shift to my right, as far away from her as I can get. Look forward but feel her eyes boring into my cheek. "You got that hotel room voucher from the airline, right? You might still be able to use it, get some sleep before your flight."

"But there's only one step left to go." She looks totally confused and totally determined, all at the same time. "We *have* to finish."

"You're tired," I say again. I do not want to get pulled into a discussion about this. "And if the hotel won't take the voucher after midnight, let me spot you. I'll feel better knowing you're safe. It might not be a big, fancy room — I'm not some rich asshole from Westchester, so my generosity can only go so far." Why did I say *that*? "But I can make sure you have somewhere to crash."

"What's the matter with you?" We're making eye contact through our reflections in the window opposite as the lights of the subway tunnel flash past. Her expression is so hurt, so confused, I can barely handle it. The drunk yuppie is mumbling about why one should never let a "proxy" make a call on "depreciation." Whatever that means.

"Nothing's the matter with me," I say. "I just ... think we should stop."

We keep staring at each other through the window, the train slowing down to the next station.

Bing bong. "This is a Bronx-bound D train. The next stop is Thirty-Fourth Street–Herald Square."

The train lurches to a stop with a hiss that sounds despairing, the momentum of the train forcing Charlotte to lean into me. "Fine. We were getting off here anyway."

She's on her feet, going for the doors, which are sliding open. It's after one in the morning, so there's no one to slow her down. I watch her leave — a stranded British girl, stuck on a subway train on Christmas Day, who's just been told to get lost by her only friend in New York. I should just let her go.

But I'm rising up off my seat, because — in spite of everything — I actually don't want to be away from her.

"Char —"

I stop dead at the sound of a whine behind me, turning on my heels. Mistake! I was so wrapped up in my sort of fight with Charlotte that I almost forgot the pup.

"Oh, come here, girl," I tell her, picking up the tote bag. "I'm sorry. I didn't mean to leave you."

Bing bong!

"Stand clear of the closing doors, please."

"Wha —"

Even as I'm turning back around, I know that I'm not going to make it. The doors are already sliding shut.

Crap!

I see Charlotte on the platform. She's walking away from the train, gesturing with one hand. Talking to me, without realizing that I'm not behind her. Probably cursing me out for cutting our stepping short.

The doors slam together, trapping me inside, her on the platform. The sound makes her realize I'm not there, finally, and she turns around. We just stare at each other as the D train lurches away from the platform, heading toward Forty-Second Street.

I run to the door and press my free hand on the window, wanting to tell her — what?

Wait for me?

I think I might actually love you?

But there's no time. Before I can get my act together, I'm plunged back into the dark of the subway tunnel.

I pull a whining Mistake closer to me and slump back on the bench as the yuppie suddenly startles awake, looking alarmed.

I can't believe this. Charlotte wandered into my life earlier today. Now, I'm being dragged out of hers!

~ CHAPTER ELEVEN ~

CHARLOTTE

1:10 A.M.

"Stand clear of the closing doors, please."

"Seriously," I'm saying to Anthony as I step onto the platform, "you're happy to stop now? When we've just got one step left to take? I'm not even OCD, but that makes me —"

Something about the sound of the doors sliding shut, clattering together, makes me turn around. When I do, I see that Anthony's still on the train, holding the tote bag with Mistake. He's heard the announcement but has not moved for the door.

I feel my shoulders slump. We look at each other for the two or three seconds that the train stays in the station. Anthony takes a step to the door but doesn't say or mouth anything.

Then the train lurches off toward Forty-Second Street.

He's trapped on the train. Accidentally? Or — on purpose?

There's one way to get the answer. I reach into my bag to take out my mobile but have just unlocked the home screen when I remember that I never got Anthony's number. I've hardly needed it tonight, because we've spent, probably, a grand total of eleven minutes apart from each other since I threw the bloody *Ten Easy Steps* book at him — the incident that got me into this mess in the first place.

Okay, this is not a total disaster. He'll just get off at Forty-Second Street, hop on the Brooklyn-bound train and come back. If he wants to come back.

Obviously, that's what he's going to do, right? I refuse to think about the other option right now. I can't believe that the last I'll see of Anthony is his stunned face, as the train pulled out of the Thirty-Fourth Street station. So I go upstairs and cross over to the Brooklyn-bound platform, where I sit down at a bench, hoping I'm in the right place. (He would take one of the orange trains back, right? There's no reason he'd switch to the yellow — or something else entirely? *God, I wish I'd spent more time in the city!*)

I wait five minutes. An F train pulls in, stops and discharges three passengers — none of them Anthony. The doors close, and it grinds back into the tunnel.

In the silence that follows, I swallow hard. It's niggling at me, no matter how much I don't want to think about it.

Was this an accident?

Okay — think it through, Charlotte …

But it's hard for me to think it through right now, because it all seemed so strange.

Why did he want to stop doing the steps?

He called Colin a rich asshole from Westchester. And he was right, on at least one of those counts. But why did he say it? He was talking about "Westchester assholes," saying he wasn't one …

He wasn't one, but he could get me a hotel room. Why? Was he trying to ditch me? After everything we've been through today, together? No, that doesn't make any sense at all.

Does it?

Ten minutes pass, and two more Brooklyn-bound trains rumble into the station. Both times, not many people get off, and none of them are carrying a bulldog in a canvas tote bag.

He's not coming back.

He's ditched me here ... What the hell?!

I look up and down the platform — desolate, a little end-of-the-world-y — and wonder: if Anthony *isn't* coming back, what's my next move? I'm stranded in the middle of Manhattan, in the middle of the night, and I don't even have the phone number of the guy I would have called my best friend here. I could call Colin, maybe, if he could tear himself away from Katie ...

Wait a minute? Why is Colin feeling more familiar all of a sudden? Like I was just talking to him ... in my dream.

Ohgodohgod, I *was* thinking about Colin as I was drifting off. It's coming back to me now, the memory resuming as if a commercial break has just come to an end.

I was remembering being at Katie's party, out on that balcony, looking up at Colin — the same way I had been doing less than five hours ago, except this time, he was holding my hands, as if unable to stop himself from reaching for me. Clutching at me because he needed me to be near him, couldn't handle me being far away — and "far away" was classed as anything farther than three feet. He was telling me that he had been an idiot for getting with Katie, and that he actually *did* say it back when we were at Rockefeller Center. I hadn't imagined it. He loved me.

And I had said ... Oh, God, what did I say?

What did I say?

I knew you loved me, Colin.

But in the remegined memory, I wasn't happy. Instead, I was smugly pleased that I had been right all along, that he was 'fessing up to being a knobhead. That he was regretting being so horrible to me, someone who really didn't deserve that. I was getting ready to tell him off.

But then I'd drifted off, and when I woke up, Anthony was being weird with me. As if wanting to prove that all boys are the same — moody, irritable, *annoying*.

I let out a deep sigh. I should get out of the station, right now. I can't wait around here by myself. I hold my tote bag tight to my side and sprint out, emerging onto Herald Square. I've only been here like twice since I arrived, but it still seems crazy how deserted it is. Lane after lane of roads so empty, so silent, that when a car does roll past me, the sound of the engine makes me jump. The streetlights shred the night, making everything absurdly visible, but I'm grateful for them — it's less scary this way.

For a second, I think about going back to Bensonhurst, waking his family up at two in the morning, explaining that we got separated. I'd get his number, call him and ask if he's okay — after I've called him a git for ditching me! But let's be serious: any guy that would just leave a girl by herself, after one in the morning, in the middle of Manhattan — on *Christmas Day* — that guy's not picking up the phone. And as furious as I am with him, I don't want to make things weird with his family. I let him see all the sides of me, and he *ran*.

What an arsehole!

But what *happened*? Why did he suddenly get so arsey with me? Why did he suddenly decide that he didn't want to do the final step, that he was actually more than happy to throw some money at his Charlotte problem and put me away in a hotel until my flight tomorrow? I mean, I was dozing, half asleep at the time — how could I have upset a boy while I was *not totally conscious*?

I run my hands through my hair, then shake my head and try to wake myself up. But my exhaustion is like a giant, slimy hand pushing at the back of my head. I just want to sleep. I just want to go home. I just want to find Anthony and ask him, what the *hell* was that about? The early hours of Christmas morning, and you ditch me — *and* steal our dog?

I walk in one direction, then the other, not really sure *where* I'm going to go. Then I turn to look back in the direction of Thirty-Fourth Street–Herald Square station, hoping to see Anthony and Mistake jogging toward me. But the street is deserted, the shuttered windows of Macy's looking so severe that the night is starting to feel a little dystopian.

He's not coming back. He's gone.

✳

I spend a few minutes idly walking along Thirty-Fourth Street, trying not to think about how Midtown is looking a bit apocalyptic, what with it being so empty of people and traffic at this time of night. Every single taxi seems to crawl by, and I imagine the drivers inside looking left and right desperately, hoping to see some survivors.

So, what now? The last step said to "do something to help yourself gain perspective," but the only perspective I have right now is of an empty, dark city. An empty, dark city where — *apparently* — I don't have any friends at all. Not the girls from Sacred Heart — the kind of girls who'll run off with my boyfriend the minute we break up — and not Anthony, my companion on what I'm starting to think was a journey to nowhere.

You know what? Screw him, I'm not going to just stand around in the cold and wait for him to grace me with his presence.

I'm going to do the thing I was planning to do when I got off the train.

Go to the Empire State Building.

Trumpets blare from within my tote bag. My mobile — a text-message alert! Maybe Anthony has somehow figured out my number? It wouldn't be *that* hard to do.

But it's just a text from the airline, informing me that due to all the delays and cancellations, they've laid on extra emergency flights to London. The next one takes off at five in the morning, and my name is on the list. I could actually be home for Christmas dinner. I won't have to avoid *Doctor Who* spoilers for a day! *This* is a Christmas miracle!

But if I do this — if I set off for the airport right now — Anthony won't ever find me, if he even doubles back (and why would he do that if ditching me was his actual intention?). I'll *never* see him again — my Day Friend in New York, who I was starting to hope might become something more. I might be going home to my family, who I love, but I know the only thing I'll really be feeling is the absence of ... the absence of what? Of Anthony? No, that can't be right, I barely know him.

I guess I'll be thinking about what might have been.

I turn around to stare at the station entrance, standing stock-still and giving my Day Friend as much time as possible to emerge onto the street, carrying our dog in his arms and an apology on his face. But no one's coming out of the station.

I check my watch, see that it's almost quarter to two.

If I'm never coming back, there's no way I'm leaving without taking Step Ten. And if the hours I looked up on my mobile are to be believed, the observation deck closes at two — every night.

I turn and walk away from the station, in the direction of Fifth Avenue.

~ CHAPTER TWELVE ~

ANTHONY

1:12 A.M.

Goddamnit, how could I be such an idiot?

Charlotte's going to think I ditched her on purpose, especially after I made such a big deal about paying for her room and not bothering with the final step. She probably didn't even realize what she'd said — to her, it had to have seemed like I turned into an asshole in an instant.

I know that Charlotte babbling about Colin while she's half asleep does not mean that she actually wants to get back with him.

I sit down on the train bench with Mistake, holding her close to me while I try to figure out my next move. The next stop is Forty-Second Street, and I can get off and double back. Charlotte might take some time to get herself together. She could still be there by the time I make it back to Herald Square …

In the tunnel, a Brooklyn-bound train passes mine, going in the other direction. *It's fine, it's fine,* I tell myself. *I might have to wait at Forty-Second Street for a few minutes, but she'll totally wait for me to double back. She'll be there.*

But somehow, I'm getting the feeling that she won't be — that she'll see my sudden disappearance as me ditching her. Ditching her and stealing our dog. I try to calm down, try to convince myself that I'm overreacting, but I can't help it — this is a total disaster. This amazing night is going to shit right at the end. And, unlike my last relationship, it is all my fault, because *I'm* the one who's done the screwing up. Here was a nice, smart, kind and down-to-earth girl — who seemed to like me, who seemed to *get* me, who *chose* to spend her last night in the city with me. And right when we were bringing that night — which, all things considered, has been kind of perfect — to a close, I go and ruin it by saying something that is Total Bollocks.

I don't even know if I'm using that right, but I'm actually starting to talk like her in my head! *Come on, train, get to Forty-Second Street. Please!* For once, I'd like something to go right. Because, if it doesn't, and I don't get back to Thirty-Fourth Street–Herald Square soon, I'll have lost Charlotte forever. I'll have no shot at finding her, because — idiot that I am — I didn't even get her last name. I can't look her up on Instagram or anything. My "missed connections" post on Craigslist would probably say something like, "Your name is Charlotte, and you're British. You're funny when you swear, and you were scared of sledding until you actually tried it. We had the best night ever, and I'm the doofus who let you get off the train."

The train that I'm stuck on slows to a stop and sits in the tunnel. The driver gets on the PA system and informs us — well, me, as I'm the only conscious passenger on this car — that there's a sick passenger on the train in front of us, who's being attended to, and we'll be stuck here a few minutes.

Mistake looks up at me and whimpers.

"We're going to find her," I whisper.

✳

"I know, I know," I gasp to Mistake. I'm out of breath from running, and the pup is yapping with annoyance at how hard I'm clutching her to my chest. Either she fears that I'm going to drop her, or the feel of my racing heart against her ear is bothering her. "It'll all be worth it if she's there."

God, I hope Charlotte's still there.

According to my phone's clock, half an hour has passed since Charlotte and I got separated by the time I make it back to Herald Square. After the holdup, I just missed another Brooklyn-bound train and then waited on the platform for what felt like forever but was probably only five minutes or so.

I'm here now. Surely, Charlotte would give me half an hour?

But when I make it to the uptown platform at Thirty-Fourth Street–Herald Square, she's nowhere to be seen. I even call out to her, but all I get is my own echo bouncing back to me. I run the length of the platform, but the only person here is a dude in a field coat over a plaid shirt, so similar to mine I wonder if I've started hallucinating this whole incident. Maybe I've been asleep on the D train all along, and I'm still sitting next to Charlotte, heading uptown.

Then Mistake nips at my arm, like, *Seriously, Dad, stop running*, and I can't deny anymore that this is real. This is really happening.

Charlotte is not here.

I stop, take a seat on the bench and let Mistake settle down. I've blown it. I'm such a tool. Charlotte wasn't my chance at getting over Maya, she wasn't my redemption, she wasn't any of that. She was a girl that I met, a girl that I liked and would have liked if I had met her on my very best day.

And now, I've lost her.

Mistake barks at me — I can't tell whether she's asking to be put on the ground or telling me to snap out of it and fix this. And even though I've known Charlotte less than ten hours, I think I might actually have a shot at figuring out where she might have gone. I've just got to *think* ...

She was going somewhere, and it was around this neighborhood. Step Ten ... Step Ten ... something about "gaining perspective."

Of course. I realize where Charlotte wanted to go. It's not the first time I've come to this conclusion tonight, but, this time, I'm not annoyed — I'm psyched. Suddenly, Charlotte's lame, touristy idea seems totally and completely perfect.

I cuddle the tote bag to me, trying to sound as reassuring as possible when I tell Mistake: "Okay, girl, I'm going to need you to act like a stuffed animal right now. Can't have you wriggling and squirming and making noise ... Not if we want to get into the Empire State Building!"

*

I'm inside the lobby in two minutes, and Mistake is making me proud, lying completely still in Max's old tote bag. The ticket seller in the glass booth is a middle-aged woman, and as I approach, she's standing up, putting her phone into her pocket. I get the sinking feeling that she's shutting down for the day. When she sees me and Mistake trotting up to her, she makes a "sorry" face.

"Just tell me," I gasp, "did a British girl come by here in the last few minutes? Have you seen her leave?"

"We get a lot of tourists, honey," she says, going back to inspecting her purse. Her badge says "Paula."

"Please, ma'am. It's nearly two a.m. on Christmas Day. There can't have been *so* many people that you can't remember."

I don't know if it's the crack in my voice or the yap that Mistake puts in — as if to say, "Hey, lady, the boy's in love!" — but when Paula looks at me again, she's taking me more seriously. And why not? Nobody shows up at the Empire State Building at two on Christmas morning — with a puppy — asking about a British girl unless they have a really good reason!

She looks at me, and she must see the desperation on my face, because she nods and starts tapping on the keyboard in front of her. "We did have one come by," she says. "Few minutes ago." She reaches down to retrieve the ticket she's printed for me, as I shove some bills across to her. I'm overpaying for this visit, and I don't care one bit.

Paula tells me that I have ten minutes, no more. She's got a home to go to.

Paula, I love you. Not as much as I love Charlotte, but you're a close second right now!

I take two elevators up to the observation deck, barely waiting for the doors to open before I jump out. It's almost deserted, apart from the old couple to my left. They each have an arm around the other and are wearing matching woolen coats and thick gloves, scarves covering half their faces. They're looking west, over the Hudson, toward New Jersey. Totally content, totally happy. But screw that: I'm looking for my *own* contentedness and happiness.

The winter chill is even fiercer this high up. The snow has returned, thick enough that Mistake burrows into the tote bag for warmth and shelter.

Where is she?

It's only now that I'm here that I think to myself, what if Charlotte's gained her perspective and taken an elevator *down*? What if we passed each other and never knew that we did?

What if she thinks I never tried to find her?

No, that can't happen. Paula's got my back, right? She'll intercept Charlotte and make sure she doesn't leave, not without me.

She has to be here. But I run all around the observation deck, totally ignoring the magnificent view flitting past me. The New York skyline might as well be made of cardboard and Styrofoam, for all the attention I'm giving it.

There's only one sight that I want to see.

And there she is, facing the Hudson, looking at — why is she looking at *New Jersey*? I know she's not from here, but come on, girl. *Whatever.* I'll run up to her and get her facing in the right direction — right at me. Once I kiss her, she'll forget that New Jersey even exists (which is the way to live, really). I touch her shoulder and —

Wrong girl.

"Sorry," I say to the woman, who I now realize is in her midthirties and, when she starts speaking, Russian. "I'm really sorry. I thought you were someone else."

And here's the strapping Russian husband, who does not seem happy at all that I was bugging his wife.

"I'm *so* sorry. Really, really, did not mean to do that. Can I take a picture of you guys? No? Well, listen, enjoy your stay in ..."

And when I cast my eyes over at the northwest corner of the deck, I trail off — because there she is. A silhouette looking uptown, toward ... Columbia. I manage to split off from the Russian couple, then stop — because as much as I want to see her and tell her everything, I also want her to make her decision on her own. No guy — not even me — should be any kind of factor in what she decides to do with *her* future. I believed that when I said it about the horrible hipster, and I believe it just as much now. If she comes back to New York, it should be because she wants to, whether I'm here or not. She's completing the last step — gaining perspective and thinking about *everything*.

I'm content to let her have this moment, for as long as she wants it to last — but Mistake has other ideas. As soon as she sniffs the air and recognizes her mom's scent, she tries to launch herself out of my arms, and when I stop her, she starts barking. Her barks are initially swallowed up by the fierce December winds gusting around the observation deck, but they eventually reach their target.

Charlotte starts to turn around. I realize how nervous I am. She looks stunned, staring at me as if she has just been asked to divide three by seventeen — as if she can't, for the life of her, figure out what I might be doing here.

But *I* know what I'm doing here. I walk right up to her, shifting our dog to one side, reaching out my free hand to take one of hers. I pull her toward me and kiss her. She kisses me back, taking two fistfuls of my jacket, pulling me close until there is barely any space between our lips, our bodies ...

Until our dog creates some, both of us leaning back to avoid her enthusiastic licks. We break apart, laughing, Charlotte reaching out to fuss over Mistake.

"You're so lucky I adore you so much, little madam!" Then she looks to the floor, biting her lip, suddenly emotional. "I waited for you. What happened? Why did you let me go?"

"I didn't mean to," I tell her, surprised I can speak at all. It feels like my heart is trying to climb out of my chest, out of my mouth and present itself to her. "I was getting Mistake together, and the doors closed ..."

"I thought you'd just decided the night was over," she whispers. She looks up, and I can see her teeth clench as she tries to keep her breathing under control. The biting cold air of the Manhattan sky has given her cheeks a pink glow that — to me, right now — lights up the night.

I lightly grab her sleeve again, pull her toward me, hold her close. "I'm so glad we found you."

She leans in and rests her forehead against my chest, still stroking Mistake's nose. "I can't believe it ... I really thought you'd ..." Now she wraps both arms around my waist, squeezes tight. "I didn't expect you to try to find me."

I remember something I've thought and said tonight. I have to tell her. She needs to know it. "Look at me ..."

She leans her head away from me, looking up. Her eyes glimmer, but the tears don't fall.

"I thought *you* had rejected me, on the train," I tell her. "You were saying something ... about Colin. You were falling asleep."

Her eyes widen. "*Colin?* That arsehole?"

I can't help laughing, and after a second, she joins in.

"I *was* thinking about him," she says, quietly. "But I think what I was really doing was letting him *go*. Letting go of the idea that he was ever that important."

I reach out and touch her cheek, and she looks up at me and smiles. "I think we're both realizing that," I say. "The people from our past ... maybe don't mean as much as the people in ..." I trail off, too chickenshit to say it.

But she's not. "Our future?"

I just nod, smiling.

She laughs, shakes her head. "God, what are we *like*?"

I lean forward, letting my lips rest on her forehead. "We're like a couple of fools, but that's okay." Her arms squeeze me tighter. Mistake nestles into both of us.

She leans her head away so she can look at me, her eyes narrowing, and I can tell that she's trying to capture a memory of something.

"You ... were saying something to me. On the train ... just before we got separated."

"I said a lot of things on the train." I kiss the top of her head, try not to shiver at the scent of lilac. "You were pretty tired."

"Can you ..." I can feel her heartbeat against my ribs. It could almost be the bass line for a dubstep track. "Can you remember what you said? I'm gutted I didn't catch it all."

I close my eyes and try to remember. I wasn't really thinking about what I was saying while I was saying it; it was a ramble, stream of consciousness.

I was just saying what felt right. That's what I should do now.

"If you had asked me earlier today, could I ever be happy again, I'd have probably laughed at you. Because I don't think I've ever felt less of myself than I did after … after what happened this afternoon. But I don't care about any of that anymore. I don't think I'm ever even going to think about it again."

I have no idea how close that was to what I said on the train, but I *do* remember how I finished up. And now that I've got a second chance at it, I have to change one thing I said.

"You know, earlier, after we had the pizza at John's, I wondered how random this night was going to get. It had been pretty ridiculous already, and there you were, on a Citi Bike, telling me to follow you. I didn't know where the heck you were going, but … I wanted to find out. That was true then, and it's true now.

"I *have* to find out — about you, about us. Every day, I want to find out —"

The very end of my ramble is cut off by the kiss she gives me, which is almost as hard as the grip she has on the back of my neck — I'm struck by the difference, the improvement, in kissing someone who you know really wants to kiss *you*. Just you.

When she stops kissing me, we're both breathing heavily. Those dimples deepen as she smiles, both of us ignoring the snow that's battering our faces.

"I love you." She says it, and I'm surprised that I'm not surprised. "It might be totally mental, but I do."

I lean forward, resting my forehead against hers. Whisper, "I'm sorry about leaving you."

She slides her hands around my hips, pulling me to her again. "No, *I'm* sorry. This wouldn't have happened if I hadn't dozed off. I hate that

I did — I don't want to miss a moment. I was just … a bit confused. All of a sudden, you were telling me that we should stop, that you'd pay for a hotel and I … I didn't know what to do."

"I liked you too much. I guess that's why it hurt so bad when I heard his name come out your mouth. I know how you felt about him."

She leans back a little to make sure that we're looking at each other — that I take her seriously when she tells me: "How I *thought* I felt about him. And you know something? If I hadn't met you, if we hadn't done … everything we've done, I'd still be thinking that what Col— what he and I were was something real. *You* showed me that it wasn't."

I'm about to say something but am interrupted by a blast of trumpets. Charlotte shakes her head, mumbling: "Probably my mum, making sure I'm okay." She takes her cell phone out of her tote bag, looks at it. Whatever it is, it stops her in her tracks, because I hear a sharp intake of breath. "Oh … it's the airline. They're pushing me to confirm whether or not I'll be on one of the extra flights they've laid on."

"Tell them yes." I say it without hesitation, and from the way she looks at me, all furrowed brows, I can tell that Charlotte is confused. "I don't want this night to end, but … you should be with your family. It's Christmas. And I actually … I want to be with mine. Thanks to you."

"What did I do?"

"You reminded me that it wasn't my family I was trying to avoid," I say. "It was me, my own grief. But that makes no sense, because I'm carrying that around with me everywhere. I can't move forward if I'm running away. And moving forward starts at home — for both of us."

"The emotional base?" she asks, saying to me something I said to her when we were at Washington Square, about the idea of "home." I can't help grinning at the fact that she remembers — because she listens.

We hear each other.

I nod at her. "Yeah, the emotional base."

She holds my eyes for a second, before the first tear falls and she looks at the ground. "But I don't want to leave ..."

"Come here." I take her left hand in my right, guide her over to the wall, to the view of the Upper West Side. Perspective. "Look."

She stares out, over the scene she was looking at when I arrived here. Just for a few seconds, then she looks back at me. "I don't get it."

I point out over the edge, at the snow-covered park spilling away from us, like a white carpet being unrolled, presenting the Upper West Side, Columbia, the next year of our lives.

"All of that is still going to be here, waiting for you to come back." I return her look, interlacing her fingers with mine. "It's not going anywhere. And neither am I. If you want us, we're yours. You know why?"

"Why?"

I lean down, kiss her once. "Because here — you will belong."

10. DO SOMETHING TO HELP YOURSELF GAIN PERSPECTIVE.

CHAPTER THIRTEEN

CHARLOTTE

2:07 A.M.

Everything after the kissing and the declarations is a blur. I feel so light, so happily dizzy, that it's like I'm floating down from the top of the Empire State Building, back to Thirty-Fourth Street. Once we're there, Anthony instantly steps into the street and raises his hand. I reach out to restrain him.

"It's okay," he says. "You need to get home to your family, to your sisters. It's okay. Come on, let's hurry."

I laugh at him. "I'm not trying to get out of going home. I just …"

He leans down to find my eyes, looking both suspicious and amused. "What is it?"

"Could you let *me* hail the cab?" I look away, embarrassed at how much this means to me. I've never hailed one in New York before, and I'm strangely struck by the urge to go through it as a kind of rite of passage. Anthony just smiles, takes a step back:

"The city is yours, m'lady."

And right at this moment, it feels like it really is … until two cabs totally ignore me. I give Anthony a look, start to step back to let him do it.

"No, no, no," he says, gently nudging me back to the curb. "A cab is a New Yorker's *right*. You have to raise your hand like you *expect* it to stop — like it hasn't even occurred to you that it wouldn't."

I sigh, turn back to the street. A lone pair of headlights slices through the New York night, a block up Thirty-Fourth. *This is yours*, I tell myself. *You got this.*

I step one foot off the curb, raise my hand to hail the cab. I look directly at it, like I'm in a staring contest with the headlights and ...

It *actually* slows, stops and veers over to me. As Anthony and I get in, I try not to do a little happy dance. Anthony nudges my arm.

"You are one of us now," he says.

It feels true. It feels brilliant.

✳

Five minutes later, we're in the cab, heading toward JFK, and I'm feeling exhilarated and exhausted (exhilausted!). We're holding hands, lazily repositioning our fingers in a rhythm that is slow and haphazard, and yet we never miss a beat, never get tangled.

It's probably not at all necessary — not after everything we've done and said tonight — but I still feel the need to reach out with my free hand, pinch his chin and turn his face to me.

"I'm coming back for you."

He makes a scared face. "You make it sound like you're hunting me."

Most times tonight, we've laughed and joked with each other, and it's been great. But now, I'm not in the mood to laugh. Time to be serious. "You know what I mean."

He looks back at me, his face serious, his eyes not blinking. "I know. I told you, I'll be waiting — and so will the city."

"Are you sure you can do this?" I ask, shifting to look up at him. "Are you sure you can wait?"

"Are *you*?"

My answer comes instantly, no hesitation. "I don't know where this is going but … I want to find out."

He smiles, leans across and kisses me again. I feel a tear weave its way between our lips. I don't know if it's his or if it's mine. I don't care.

Anthony breaks the kiss, leans back and looks at me. Deadly serious again. "If we are going to do this," he says, "then there's something *very important* that we have to do first. There's something I've just gotta know …"

I feel my chest tighten as I wonder, what is it he's going to ask?

"What's your last name?"

Has that seriously not come up until now?

I laugh, and tell him my name. "It's Cheshire."

He smiles, nods, like it makes sense. "One more question … This one's a bit, uh … forward, I guess."

I try not to look as flustered as I feel, imagining what on earth he could possibly be gearing up to ask.

"Can I get your number?"

✳

The next thing I know, I've got a new boarding pass in one hand and am holding Anthony's with the other. Mistake, on her lead, walks between us but slowly — the poor pup is knackered.

We're walking toward Security, and I'm feeling as much excitement about being home as I am hesitation and dread at leaving Anthony. It's not that I fear that he'll find someone else if I'm not here, that he'll cheat on me the way his ex did. It's more that now that my departure is looming, the prospect suddenly inescapable, I just don't want to be apart from him.

And now, we've reached the start of the mazy line that leads to Security. Ahead are other bleary-eyed, frazzled Europeans, staggering toward flights that they were not expecting to take.

"So …" When I look at him, I can tell Anthony doesn't really have anything more to say right now.

I reach down into my tote bag and take out *Get Over Your Ex in Ten Easy Steps* — the book that got us both into amusing, ridiculous, legal and, eventually, wonderful trouble tonight. "Guess we don't need this anymore, huh?"

He smiles, takes it from me, turns it over in his hands. Shakes his head. "I can't believe it actually worked."

"Perhaps we should leave it for someone else to find? You never know, someone on one of the later flights might be in need of the same help that we were."

He smiles again, looking around. His eyes alight on a row of seats — four of them — just before the start of Security. He walks over to them and bends to place the book on the third seat. When he stands up, his face is solemn, but there is a gentle smile on his lips. He puts his hand against his chest, then looks at me, his eyebrows raised, like, *What are you waiting for?*

I mimic his pose. He turns back to the book. "May you heal more hearts this Christmas — just … try to make sure the next couple doesn't get picked up by cops!"

I let out a sharp laugh, and then we both nod solemnly and wave our goodbyes to the book. He walks back to the line and takes my hand again. He squeezes. "You got my number, right?"

I grin at him. "And your email and your Instagram. There's no escaping me, Monteleone!"

"I'm not running anywhere."

He kisses me again, and I'm thinking those seven hours or so between us meeting and us first kissing was time that we wasted.

We break the kiss when Mistake's lead gets tangled around my legs. The pup is walking in and out of them and has me pretty well tied up. Anthony's laughing as he kneels down to get to work on setting me free — as if he hasn't done enough of that already today.

"I think she's going to miss you almost as much as I will," he says.

I keep my response light — if I go for meaningful or sincere, I think I might cry. "Yeah, you'd better miss me."

"I will. You're amazing."

I'm looking down at him, but what I'm seeing is myself, through Anthony's eyes. The girl he met tonight is a girl who was down but eventually got up and took on a city — with him right alongside her. A girl who didn't know where she was going or where she wanted to go, who felt she might not belong anywhere and had the strength to answer those questions for herself. That's the version of me I'm taking home to London. And she's the version of me I'll be bringing back here in about eight months.

Anthony knew she was there, all along.

9. ~~SEE YOURSELF HOW SOMEONE ELSE SEES YOU.~~

I reach down and lightly stroke the top of his head, letting my hand slide down the back of his neck. "Thank you."

When he looks up at me, he initially seems confused. But only for a second. He nods and smiles, his eyes saying everything: *I'll miss you. I can't wait to see you again.* After he finishes untangling Mistake, he picks her up.

"Come on, little lady, say bye to Mommy."

I take her from him and cuddle her close, asking Anthony: "Do you think you'll keep her?"

"Of course," he says. "She's *our* dog."

I hand our dog back to him, giving her one last pat on the head as I promise her that I'll see her soon. To Anthony:

"I'll follow you as soon as I get home." Okay — (a) that sounds creepy, and (b) it's a bit of a paradox. "You know, like, on Instagram." Ugh! Why is it now, at the end of a perfect night, that I'm saying lame stuff again? I think it'd be best if I don't say anything more, so I simply tell Anthony, "Bye," and turn to the security line and try to outrun my lame farewell. But I can't escape my embarrassment — I have to carry my flaming cheeks with me wherever I go.

I'm just within sight of the X-ray machine, beginning to kneel down so I can unlace my boots, when I hear a man's voice saying, "Sir, you can't —"

I don't hear anything else, because my hand's been taken in someone else's — I don't need to look to know whose — and I'm being kissed.

Being kissed so perfectly that, when I pull away, I'm a little dizzy, my legs feeling like they're made of paper. I'm giddy all over again, trying to get used to how everything's feeling so *perfect* all of a sudden …

Until the sour-faced TSA agent who's appeared behind Anthony clears his throat and asks "sir" if he has a boarding pass. Because if he doesn't have a boarding pass, he's "got no business being in this part of the airport."

I give Anthony's hand one last squeeze as I look up at him. For about three seconds, I try to think of what on earth I can say that will make this moment as meaningful as it can possibly be, until I realize: There's nothing more for us to say today. We've said it all.

I lift his hand to my lips, giving the back of it a gentle kiss. To him, I give a smile. Then I turn around and resume my journey home, thinking, *Just eight months, and I'll be back …*

… and Anthony will be waiting.

~ EPILOGUE ~

CHARLOTTE

JANUARY 2ND

"Charlotte! Package for you!"

In my bedroom back home, I snap my book closed and toss it toward the foot of my bed. Eighty pages into *Payback* — I finally bought a copy after I landed at Heathrow — and I still haven't found out why Donny "HAS IT COMING."

I head out of my room and down the stairs. Mum is in the front passage, holding a parcel. Beside her is Emma, staring at it as if she's expecting to develop X-ray vision any second now. My littlest sister has always been super nosy.

"What is it, Lot, what is it?" she asks, coming to stand beside me when I take the parcel from Mum. The first thing I see is the five-digit New York postcode, and then the family name "Monteleone."

"It's for me," I say, sticking my tongue out at her and turning around to head back upstairs, taking them two at a time, then running into my bedroom, closing the door so quickly, it slams into the frame, making the whole house shake. "Sorry!" I shout to Mum.

I set the parcel down on my bed and open it up. Inside is a chaos of beautiful turquoise tissue wrapping paper, which tickles my hands as I move it aside. Beneath is a plain scarf in a shade of blue I recognize as Columbia blue. Pinned to one edge is a photograph of Anthony in the kitchen of his family's home. He's sitting at the table, with Mistake on his lap — our dog staring right down the lens, stretching forward as if she's about to try and eat it. It's only been a week or so, but I can't believe how much I miss them both.

On the other side of the photo is a note, in handwriting I know that I will one day recognize as unmistakably his.

I know it's not Christmas anymore, but I need no reason to buy you a gift. Whatever gift I give you would be nothing compared to what you've given me (and I don't just mean Mistake!).

See you this summer.
M & A xx

I grin at the piece of paper like a nutter, enjoying the feeling of having a chest full to bursting — and not the painful kind of bursting. It's all stretching out before me now. A school and a city where I will belong, as New Charlotte. New Charlotte is going to make New York her home, at least for a while. I don't know where this Story goes or how it ends …

But I want to find out.

ACKNOWLEDGMENTS

Few books are solely the work of those whose name(s) is (are) on the cover, and this one is no exception. Huge thanks to Samantha Noonan, Charles Nettleton, Chris Snowdon and Clare Hutton for all their great suggestions as this manuscript took shape; and to Kate Egan at KCP Loft for having insights that improved the book even further. Thanks, also, to Alexandra Devlin, Harim Yim, Rachel Richardson, Allison Hellegers and Alex Webb at Rights People for championing the book around the world! And now, like with the book itself, we will divide the remainder of this love-fest into two!

JAMES NOBLE is an editor who also writes under a variety of pseudonyms. He was born and raised in London. He went to primary and secondary school in London. He went to college in London. He got his first — and only, and current — publishing job in London. He has intermediate Cockney rhyming slang, loves pie and mash (though he recoils at the mere mention of jellied eels), and never forgets to "mind the gap." But he still loses far too much of far too many days daydreaming about what it'd be like to live in New York.

Love and gratitude to my mum and dad, Debbie and Jimmy, my brothers, John and Joe (and Emma!), and to all the wild branches (Bailey and Brennan) of my family tree; to the dear friends and creative bravehearts from whom I constantly learn — most especially Lila, for always setting the example, and Stephanie, for inviting me to work on this with her!

STEPHANIE ELLIOTT is a book editor who moved to New York immediately after college. She has never been mugged, ridden a Citi Bike or been harassed by a rogue Elmo in Times Square (though one did get a little salty with her, once). She feels strongly that bialys are better than bagels, yellow cabs are better than Ubers and pizza must NEVER be eaten with a fork. She loves visiting London, where people are SO polite! She lives in Brooklyn with her husband and five-year-old daughter.

Love and thanks to my parents, my supportive friends, the Elliotts, the Lanes and the always-fascinating city of New York, for providing endless inspiration. Particularly big hugs to Dan and Maggie, my two loves who are always up for exploring the city with me. And a special thanks to James, for his love of this story and his amazing contributions!

Coming soon …

Kiss Me in PARIS

by
Catherine Rider

Available in 2018

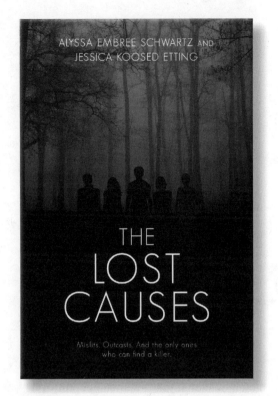

COMPULSIVELY READABLE, *THE LOST CAUSES* SWEEPS READERS INTO THE PLACE WHERE SCIENCE FICTION AND MYSTERY MEET, ENDING ON A DROP-DEAD CLIFFHANGER THAT WILL LEAVE THEM LONGING FOR MORE.

kcploft.com

Kim Turrisi

Just a

After you lose everything ...

Normal

what's left?

Tuesday

Praise for *Just a Normal Tuesday*

"There is grief and there is grace, and this book is full of both. A look at love, loss, and learning to live with questions that have no answers. Kim Turrisi is an exquisite new voice."

— Martha Brockenbrough,
    author of THE GAME OF LOVE AND DEATH

KCP Loft

kcploft.com

FAME. LOVE. FRIENDS. PICK ANY TWO.

MARIE POWELL
& JEFF NORTON

"You're the drummer," she said to herself. "It's your job to keep them on beat. To hold it all together."

But how the bloody hell was she supposed to do that?

kcploft.com

What if one touch could tell you everything?

ZENN DIAGRAM

WENDY BRANT

"Brant's debut is an **absolute treat**."
— *Booklist*, starred review

"Readers who love **quirky, character-driven romances**, such as John Green's *An Abundance of Katherines* and **heartstring-yanking melodrama** in the vein of Lauren Oliver's YA books will enjoy this novel ..."
— *School Library Journal*

KCP Loft

kcploft.com

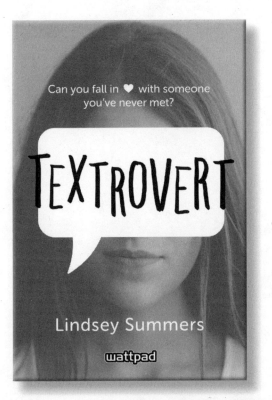

Can you fall in ♥ with someone you've never met?

TeXTROVeRT

Lindsey Summers

wattpad

DON'T MISS THE DEBUT NOVEL FROM WATTPAD SENSATION
DoNotMicrowave

KCP Loft

kcploft.com